The Forbidden Doors Series

FORBIDDEN ● DOORS

the society

BILL MYERS

TYNDALE KIDS

Tyndale House Publishers, Inc.   Wheaton, Illinois

Visit the exciting Web site for kids at www.cool2read.com
and the Forbidden Doors Web site at
www.forbiddendoors.com

ISBN 0-8423-3987-6, mass paper

Printed in the United States of America

07   06   05
10   9   8   7   6

*This series is
dedicated to
Karen Ball,
whose vision
and persistence
made it possible.*

For we are not fighting against people made of flesh and blood, but against persons without bodies—the evil rulers of the unseen world, those mighty satanic beings and great evil princes of darkness who rule this world; and against huge numbers of wicked spirits in the spirit world. So use every piece of God's armor to resist the enemy whenever he attacks, and when it is all over, you will still be standing up.

Ephesians 6:12-13

1

*R*ebecca's lungs burned. They screamed for more air; they begged her to slow down. But she wouldn't. She pushed herself. She ran for all she was worth. She had to.

There was no sound. She saw a few kids standing along the track, opening their mouths and shouting encouragement. She saw them clapping their hands and cheering her on. But she couldn't hear them. All she heard was her own gasps for breath . . . the faint crunch of gravel under her track shoes.

Several yards ahead ran Julie Mitchell—the team's shining hope for all-State. She had a grace and style that made Rebecca feel like, well, like a deranged platypus. Whatever that was.

But that was OK; Becka wasn't running against Julie. She was running against something else.

"It's Dad . . ."

For the thousandth time, she saw her mom's red nose and puffy eyes and heard her voice echoing inside her head. *"They found his plane in the jungle. He made it through the crash, but . . ."*

Becka bore down harder; she ran faster. Her lungs were going to explode, but she kept going.

"You've got . . . to accept it," her mom's voice stammered. *"He's gone, sweetheart. He was either attacked by wild animals or . . . or . . ."*

Becka dug her cleats in deeper. She stretched her legs out farther. She knew the "or . . . or . . ." was a tribe of South American Indians in that region. A tribe notorious for its fierceness and for its use of black magic.

The back of Becka's throat ached. Not

because of the running. It was because of the tears. And the rage. Why?! Why had God let this happen? Why had God let him die? He was such a good man, trying to do such good things.

Angrily she swiped at her eyes. Her legs were turning into rubber. Losing feeling. Losing control. And still she pushed herself. She had closed the gap with Julie and was practically beside her now. The finish line waited a dozen meters ahead.

Trying out for the track team hadn't been Becka's idea. It was her mom's. "To help you fit in," she'd said.

Fit in. What a joke. Rebecca had spent most of her life living in the villages of Brazil with her mom, her little brother, and a father who flew his plane in and out of the jungle for humanitarian and mission groups. And now, suddenly, she was expected to fit in. Here? In Crescent Bay, California? Here, where everybody had perfect skin, perfect bodies, perfect teeth? And let's not forget all the latest fashions, right out of *Mademoiselle* or *Cosmopolitan* or whatever it was they read. Fashions that made Becka feel like she bought her clothes right out of *Popular Mechanics*.

That last thought pushed her over the edge. She tried too hard, stretched too far.

Her legs, which had already lost feeling, suddenly had minds of their own. The left one twisted, then gave out all together.

It was like a slow-motion movie that part of Becka watched as she pitched forward. For a second, she almost caught her balance. Almost, but not quite. She stumbled and continued falling toward the track. There was nothing she could do—only put out her hands and raise her head so the crushed red gravel would not scrape her face. Knees and elbows, yes. But not her face.

As if it really mattered.

She hit the track and skidded forward, but she didn't feel any pain. Not yet. The pain would come a second or two later. Right now, all she felt was shame. And embarrassment. Already the humiliation was sending blood racing to her cheeks and to her ears.

Yes sir, just another day in the life of Rebecca Williams, the new kid moron.

~

As soon as Becka's little brother, Scott, walked into the bookstore, he knew something was wrong. It wasn't like he was frightened or nervous or anything. It had nothing to do with what he felt. It had everything to do with the place.

It was wrong.

But why? It certainly was cheery enough. Bright sunlight streaming through the sky-lights. Aqua blue carpet. Soft white shelves with rows and rows of colorful books. Then there was the background music—flutes and wind chimes.

But still . . .

"You coming or what?" It was Darryl. Scott had met him a couple of days ago at lunch. Darryl wasn't the tallest or best-looking kid in school—actually, he was about the shortest and nerdiest. His voice was so high you were never sure if it was him talking or someone opening a squeaky cupboard. Oh, and one other thing. Darryl sniffed. About every thirty seconds. You could set your watch by it. Something about allergies or hay fever or something.

But at least he was friendly. And as the new kid, Scott couldn't be too picky who he hung with. New kids had to take what new kids could get.

For the past day or so, Darryl had been telling Scott all about the Society—a secret group that met in the back of The Ascension Bookshop after school. Only the coolest and most popular kids could join. (Scott wasn't sure he bought this "coolest and most popular" bit, since they'd let Darryl be a member. But he didn't want to hurt the little guy's feelings, so he let it go.)

"Hey, Priscilla," Darryl called as they walked past the counter toward the back of the Bookshop.

"Hey, yourself," a handsome, middle-aged woman said. She didn't bother to look from her magazine until the two boys passed. When she glanced up and saw Scott, a scowl crossed her face. She seemed to dislike him immediately. He hadn't said a thing; he hadn't done a thing. But that didn't matter. There was something about him that troubled her—a lot.

Scott was oblivious to her reaction as he followed Darryl toward the hallway at the back of the store.

So far his first week at Crescent Bay had been pretty good. No fights. No broken noses. A minimal amount of death threats. But that's the way it was with Scott. Unlike his older sister, Scott always fit in. It probably had something to do with his sense of humor. Scott was a lot like his dad in that department: He had a mischievous grin and a snappy comeback for almost any situation.

Scott was like his dad in another way, too. He had a deep faith in God. The whole family did. But it wasn't some sort of rules or regulations thing. And it definitely wasn't anything weird. It was just your basic God's-the-boss-so-go-to-church-and-try-to-make-the-world-a-better-place faith.

But sometimes that faith . . . well, sometimes it allowed Scott to feel things. Deep things.

Like now.

As he and Darryl entered the hallway, Scott brushed against a large hoop decorated with what looked like eagle feathers. He ducked to the side only to run smack-dab into a set of wooden wind chimes. They clanked and clanged noisily. Lately, Scott hadn't been the most graceful of persons. It probably had something to do with growing two inches in the last three months. He was still shorter than Becka—a fact she brought up to him on a regular basis—but he was gaining on her by the week.

As they continued down the hall, Scott noticed a number of trinkets and lockets hanging on the wall. He couldn't put his finger on it, but they looked strangely familiar.

Then he noticed something else. Frowning, he glanced around. Was it his imagination, or was it getting colder? There were no windows, open or otherwise, anywhere close by.

Something inside him began to whisper, "*Stop. . . . Turn around. . . . Go back. . . .*"

But why? Nothing was wrong. It was just a hallway. Just a bookshop.

"Here we go." Darryl gave a loud sniff as he slowed in front of the last door. He smiled, pushed up his glasses, and knocked lightly.

No answer.

"Well, it doesn't look like anybody's home," Scott said, his voice cracking in gratitude. "I guess we'd better—"

"Don't be stupid," Darryl said, reaching for the knob. "They always meet on Fridays."

Cautiously, he pushed the door open.

It was pitch-black inside. Well, except for the dozen or so candles burning around a table. And the faces illuminated by the candles. Faces Scott had seen at school. They were all staring intently at something on the table. Scott squinted in the darkness, making out some kind of board game with a bunch of letters and symbols on it. Two of the kids had their hands on a little plastic pointer that was moving back and forth across the board.

"What's that?" Scott whispered.

"What do you think it is?" Darryl whispered back. "It's a Ouija board."

"A what?"

"You use it to spell out words. You know, it tells you about the future and stuff."

Scott looked at him skeptically.

"No kidding," Darryl squeaked. Scott gri-

8

maced. Even when the guy whispered his voice sounded like a rusty hinge. Darryl continued, watching the others. "The pointer moves to those letters on the board, spelling out answers to anything you ask."

"No way," Scott scorned. As far as he could tell, the pointer moved on the board because it was pushed by the two kids whose hands were on it: a big, meaty fellow in a tank top and a chubby girl dressed all in black. "Those two, they're the ones moving it."

Darryl didn't answer. He just sniffed and stepped into the room. Scott wasn't crazy about following, but he walked in after him.

And—just like that—the plastic pointer stopped. One minute the little pointer was scooting around the board, spelling out words. The next, it came to a complete stop.

"Hey," a pretty girl complained, pushing her long red hair back. "What's wrong?"

"I don't know," the meaty guy answered. He turned to his partner, the girl in black. "Are you stopping it?"

"Not me," she said. And then, slowly turning her head toward the door, she nailed Scott with an icy look. "It's him."

Every eye in the room turned to Scott.

He raised his hand. "Hi there," he croaked, trying to smile.

Nobody smiled back.

"Ask it," the redhead demanded. "Ask it if he's the reason it's not answering."

"Yeah," the meaty guy agreed.

The girl in black tilted back her head and closed her eyes. Her hair was short and jet black—an obvious dye job. "Please show us," she said more dramatically than Scott thought necessary. "Show us the reason for your silence."

Everyone turned to the plastic pointer. Waiting. Watching.

Nothing happened.

Scott tried to swallow, but at the moment, there wasn't much left in his mouth to swallow.

Suddenly the pointer started moving. Faster than before. In fact, both the girl and the meaty guy looked down in surprise as it darted from letter to letter, barely pausing at one before shooting to the next. In a matter of seconds it had spelled out:

D-E-A-T-H

Then it stopped. Abruptly.

Everyone waited in silence. Afraid to move. Afraid to break the spell.

The girl in black cleared her throat and spoke again. But this time, a little less confidently. "What do you mean? What death?"

There was no movement. No answer.

Scott shifted slightly. He felt the chill again, but this time it was more real. It had substance. Suddenly he knew that there was something there, in the room . . . something cold and physical had actually brushed against him. He was sure of it.

Again the girl spoke. "What death? Is someone going to die? Whose death?"

No movement. More silence.

And then, just when Scott was about to say something really clever to break the tension and show everyone how silly this was, the plastic pointer zipped across the board and shot off the table.

"Look out!" Darryl cried.

Scott jumped aside, and the pointer hit the floor, barely missing his feet. He threw a look at the girl in black, certain she had flung it across the table at him.

But the expression on her face said she was just as surprised as he.

Or was she?

ᴎ

"You OK?" Julie Mitchell asked as she toweled off her thick blonde hair and approached Rebecca's gym locker.

"Sure." Rebecca winced while pulling her jeans up over her skinned knees. "Nothing a brain transplant couldn't fix."

It had been nearly an hour since her little crash-and-burn routine on the track. Of course, everyone had gathered around her, making a big deal of the whole thing, and, of course, she wanted to melt into the track and disappear. But that was an hour ago. Yesterday's news. Now most of the girls had hit the showers and were heading home.

But not Julie. It was like she purposely hung back. Becka glanced at her curiously. There was something friendly about Julie, something caring. Becka had liked her immediately . . . even though Julie was one of the best-looking kids in school.

"The team really needs you," Julie offered.

"As what? Their mascot?"

Julie grinned. She tossed her hair back and reached over to slip on a top-of-the-line, money's-no-object, designer T-shirt. "Seriously," she said, "I'm the only long-distance runner we've got. Royal High has three killers that bumped me out of State last year. But if you work and learn to concentrate, the two of us might give them a run for their money. You've got the endurance. And I've never seen anyone with such a great end sprint."

"Or such klutziness."

Julie shrugged. "You've got a point there," she teased.

Becka felt herself smiling back.

"Anybody can learn form and style," Julie
continued. "That's what coaches are for.
And if you add that to your sprint, we just
might be able to knock Royal out of State."
She rummaged in her gym basket, then bit
her lip and frowned. "Shoot . . . don't tell
me I've lost it."

Becka rubbed a towel through her hair,
then sighed. Her hair was mousy brown and
would dry three times faster than Julie's.
The reason was simple: Becka's hair was
three times thinner. Yes sir, just another one
of life's little jokes with Becka as the punch
line.

Julie's search through her basket grew
more urgent.

"What are you looking for?" Becka asked.

"My pouch . . ." There was definite concern in her voice as she continued pawing
through her clothes.

"Pouch?"

"My good luck charm."

Becka wasn't sure what Julie meant, but
she gave a quick scan along the bench.

"I just hope nobody stole it," Julie said.

Becka spotted something under the
bench. It was partially covered by towels. She
reached for it and picked up a small leather
bag with rocks or sand or something inside.

A leather string was attached at the top so it could be worn as a necklace.

"Is this it?" Becka asked.

Julie relaxed. "Yeah. Great." She took it and slipped it around her neck.

Becka watched, fighting back a wave of uneasiness. She tried to sound casual as she asked, "So, what's in it?"

"I don't know." Julie shrugged. "Some turquoise, some powders, herbs—that sort of stuff. The Ascension Lady puts them together for us—you know, for good luck."

"'Ascension Lady'?" Becka asked.

"Yeah," Julie fingered the little pouch. "'Course I don't believe in any of that stuff. But with the district preliminaries coming up, it doesn't hurt to play the odds, right?"

Becka's mind raced. She wanted to ask lots more about the pouch and this Ascension Lady, but Julie didn't give her the chance.

"Listen, we'll see you Monday," she said grabbing her backpack. "And don't be bummed, you did fine. Besides," she threw a mischievous grin over her shoulder, "we can always use a good mascot."

Becka forced a smile.

"See ya." Julie disappeared around the row of lockers and pushed open the big double doors. They slammed shut behind her with a loud *click, boooom.*

Becka didn't move. She sat, all alone . . . just her and the dripping showers.

Her smile had already faded. Not because of the pain in her knees or even because of the memories of her fall.

It was because of the pouch. She'd seen pouches like that before. In South America. But they weren't worn by pretty, rich, athletic teenagers who wanted to go to State track championships.

They were worn by witch doctors who worshiped demons.

2

hy do I always get the grunge work?" Rebecca complained. She grabbed a pile of old newspapers by their string and dragged them across the floor. Julie's leather pouch and the mysterious Ascension Lady were no longer on her mind. She was too busy shuddering at the cockroaches that scurried from under her papers and dashed toward darker quarters.

Her mom stared at the rows of stacked boxes behind them—boxes that still needed to be moved. She sighed in answer to Becka's complaint. "Honey, we've all got our jobs."

"Fine . . . then let Scotty clean out this stupid garage, and let me hook up the stereo and computer junk."

"Becka, please . . ." Mom brushed aside a tendril of gray, sweaty hair. It had been six months since Becka's dad died, but it looked like Mom had aged ten years. Maybe she had. "We all have certain skills, and Scotty's—"

"I know, Scotty's the electronic whiz kid, and I'm . . . the bag lady." Becka bit her lip. She hated being a whiner. She knew it had been a tough week for Mom—getting moved in, getting situated, trying to find work. In fact, it had been a tough week for all of them. They hadn't known a soul in the town except for some distant aunt whose name Becka couldn't even remember. But since this aunt was Mom's only relative, here they were, smack-dab in the middle of Weird Town, USA, cleaning a house that, at the moment, seemed to have been owned by the Addams Family.

"Do you think these people ever threw anything away?" Becka asked, trying to change the subject.

Mom fought to lift a half-rotted box. It wasn't heavy, just big. "Well, at least they were honest," she groaned. "The ad said the place was a fixer-upper, and this place is definitely a fixer—"

"Look out!" Rebecca cried.

The bottom of Mom's box gave way, and a dozen lightbulbs fell out, smashing and popping as they hit the concrete. Mom dropped the box with a loud *thump,* and a few more shattering *pops* followed.

The two stood a moment in stunned silence. Finally Rebecca stooped down for a closer look. "Lightbulbs?" she asked. She shook her head in amazement. "They saved their used lightbulbs?"

"Must be a hundred of 'em," Mom marveled as she peered into the box.

"I know they were ecology nuts, but . . . what's next?"

Without a word, they both turned to the stack of fifty or so boxes thrown against the back wall of the garage. Fifty or so boxes that still needed to be cleared out.

Mom pushed her hair aside, a weak grin crossing her face. "Maybe next we'll find their secret stash of used toothbrushes."

"Mom. . . ," Becka groaned.

Like Scott, Mom had a sense of humor in tough times. And it didn't get any tougher than being dog-tired and having fifty more boxes to move.

"Or how 'bout used Kleenexes—you know, nice and crispy."

"Mother . . ." Becka was weakening.

"Maybe if we're really lucky, we'll find a giant ball of used dental floss."

That was it. They both started to giggle. Neither knew what was so funny. After all, fifty boxes were still fifty boxes. No doubt about it, it had been a long week for both of them, and it didn't seem to be getting any shorter. So of course they had to laugh. Either that or cry.

Suddenly, Becka swallowed her giggles and grew still. "Listen. What was that?"

Mom quieted down and gave a listen. "I don't hear anything."

Becka scowled slightly, looking toward the boxes at the back wall. "It's stopped now. But it sounded like . . ." She hesitated, thinking she heard it again. "It sounded like a faint scraping sound—didn't you hear it?"

Mom shook her head and stared toward the boxes. Both of them stood in silence, listening, waiting—but there was nothing.

"Probably just the wind," Mom finally offered as she stooped down and started picking up the shattered bulbs.

Becka nodded and crossed to the broom and dustpan. "Yeah," she said, "probably just the wind."

~

For the past couple of hours, Scott had been able to put the Bookshop incident out of his mind. And for good reason. So far he'd mistaken his hand for a cutting board while stripping off some speaker wires and had almost blown up the TV by connecting the wrong cables to the wrong box.

Now it was a fight to the finish with the computer's modem. He was up in his room, going for the best two out of three falls with the contraption. Unfortunately, Cornelius wasn't helping much.

"BEAM ME UP, SCOTTY, BEAM ME UP."

"Not now, Cornelius, I'm busy."

The bright green bird hopped onto Scott's arm and worked his way up to Scott's right shoulder. "MAKE MY DAY. MAKE MY DAY."

Scott let out a heavy sigh. Teaching the family parrot cool phrases was fun back in the beginning. It was a great way to impress all of his Brazilian friends. The only problem was that people quit using those cool phrases a long time ago. A fact that totally

21

escaped Cornelius. The bird just kept repeating the same things over and over and over . . . and over some more. It made Scott crazy, especially when he was trying to concentrate.

"BEAM ME UP! *SQUAWK.* BEAM ME UP! BEAM ME UP!"

Scott tried to ignore him. He finished connecting the last cable, took a deep breath, and flipped the modem on.

So far so good—no power surges, no nuclear meltdowns.

He entered a chat room. His father had taught him to use chat rooms when they were in Brazil. It was a great way of communicating with the outside world. All you needed was a modem. Just hook it up, and then phone a computer and type in your message. Later you could check in to see if somebody had called up, read your message, and left an answer. Or sometimes you could type back and forth right on the spot, a kind of conversation over the computer waves.

After a few moments, the computer at the other end picked up, and a phrase suddenly popped onto Scott's screen:

Welcome to Night Light
Name?

Scott thought a moment, then typed in
what he thought was an appropriate handle:

New Kid.

There was a pause, then another phrase
appeared:

That name is not logged onto our files.
Is this your first time?
Yes.
Please select a password.

Scott gnawed on his left thumbnail as he
looked around the room for a password.
Chewing his nails was a habit he'd had all his
life. It made Mom and Becka crazy, but it
didn't bother him much—except when it
came to opening pocketknives and that sort of
thing, but hey, that's why God invented teeth.

Finally his eyes landed on his used gym
socks flung across the room. One partially
hung over his lampshade. He shrugged and
typed:

Dirty Socks.
Welcome, New Kid. Would you like to:
Leave a message?
or
Talk with someone now?

Scott reached for his computer mouse, but before he could select his answer, a flurry of green feathers leaped into his face. Cornelius had grown weary of sitting on Scott's shoulder and thought he'd fly down to the keyboard to take a little stroll. Unfortunately, he strolled across the wrong keys. Immediately the screen went blank.

"Hey!" Scott cried. But that was all he managed to get out before Cornelius reached up and began nibbling on the end of his nose.

Scott sighed. It was hard to yell when your nose was being kissed.

"Hi there. . . . Rebecca, isn't it?"

Becka froze. This was about her twentieth trip to the sidewalk with about her twentieth extra-ply, heavy-duty Glad bag filled to the brim with junk. In the beginning, when she had first stepped out of the garage and into public view, she had cared how she looked. But that was eight hours ago. Before the exhaustion. Before she became a sweaty greaseball covered in grime. Now she didn't give a rip how she looked.

Or so she thought.

She turned toward the voice and squinted into the light. The sun glared behind him so she couldn't see much—except that he was tall and had incredible shoulders.

He shifted slightly. The sun flared around his face, and now she could see his thick black hair and strong chin. She caught a glimpse of something else, too. His eyes. She'd never seen anything quite so blue.

Her face flushed instantly. Of all times to be looking like pond scum. She gave one final tug on the bag, bringing it to the curb. She was careful to keep her back to him, hoping he wouldn't recognize her. But since he already knew her name, chances of that seemed kind of slim.

"Need a hand?" he asked.

"No," she answered too quickly, almost sounding angry. She tried again. "I mean, this is the last of it for the day."

"Oh." Was it her imagination, or was there a trace of disappointment in his voice? After a moment, he continued. "The people that used to live here were really weird. Did some strange stuff."

Becka's mind raced. She knew the guy was trying to make conversation, and she wanted to help out. But at the moment, all she could think about was how awful she looked. "Well. . . ," she faltered, "we're finding some pretty weird stuff in there, that's for sure."

She reached up and discreetly tried to fluff out the stringiest part of her hair.

"If you guys ever need a hand, let me know. I just live down on the corner."

Rebecca nodded.

Another pause.

She tied another knot at the top of the bag. It didn't need it, but she had to do something. Still careful to keep her back to him, she asked, "So, uh . . . how'd you know my name?"

"I've been asking around."

"Becka?" It was Mom, calling from the garage.

"Coming," Rebecca answered. She was both mad and grateful for the excuse to get away. "Well, I've gotta go." She quickly turned and headed up the driveway. "It was nice meeting you."

"Same here—see ya."

She immediately hated herself for being such a chicken. It wasn't until she reached the garage that she realized she wasn't just a chicken. She was a brainless chicken. She hadn't even asked his name!

But he knew hers. *What'd he say? "I've been asking around"?* One eyebrow lifted, and she glanced over her shoulder in the direction he'd gone. *Hmmm . . . maybe life around here won't be so terrible after all.*

3

*B*y three o'clock the following morning, Scott had twisted his blanket and sheets into a tight little ball. He thought he'd be able to forget about the Bookshop and the Ouija board. No such luck. He just kept tossing and turning and kicking and thrashing. And the dreams just kept coming, one after another.

The latest was of his dad. Or at least his dad as Scott remembered him. Before his death.

They were playing football—just the two of them. Well, just the two of them on one side. The other side had a team of giant bruisers at the line of scrimmage just waiting to turn them into football shoe goo.

Scott shuddered as he and his dad huddled up. Not because he worried about getting tromped to death. He figured that was inevitable. He shivered because of the chill. The same chill he'd felt the day before in the bookstore.

"Scotty," his dad asked with a frown, "where's your armor?"

Scott looked to him in surprise. The man was wearing a full suit of armor, like something right out of King Arthur! It was obviously another one of his dad's little jokes. "My armor?" Scott chuckled. "Well, I, uh . . ."

"Can't play the game without your armor."

"Yeah, sure . . . I, uh . . . I guess I must have left it at the cleaners," Scott quipped, "or maybe the body shop." His dad didn't laugh. He didn't even crack a smile.

They broke from the huddle and approached the line of scrimmage. Scott glanced up at the faces of his towering opponents and gasped. There were no faces. The football helmets were there, even the face guards. But inside . . . inside there were no heads, no faces. Nothing. Just dark, ominous shadows. Scott fought back a shudder.

"Don't worry," Dad whispered. "Just run the plays."

"Plays?" Scott asked. "What plays?"

"The ones we practiced."

"Where . . . when . . . we never practiced any plays."

"Sure we did." Dad grinned. "All the time."

Scott was clueless. But before he could argue, Dad took his position over the ball. Scott had never played football in his life, but through the process of elimination, he figured if his dad was playing center, that probably made him quarterback. What a mind.

Once again Scott looked to the faces of the opposing team. Once again he only saw menacing blackness.

He took a breath. Well, it was now or never. "Ready! Set!" he yelled. He'd gotten that much from watching TV. Now what? He wasn't sure. But when all else fails, yell.

"HIKE!"

Dad snapped the ball, but to Scott's amazement, it was no longer a football. Now he was holding a small bronze shield, like in one of those old Roman gladiator movies!

Scott stared at it, frozen in surprise—but

not for long. Suddenly, the entire line of shadows charged toward him. He could hear their cleats pounding the mud; he could hear animal growls coming from their throats.

He dropped back. But they kept coming—grunting, growling, snorting like bulls. He frantically searched the field for his dad. Finally he spotted him standing on the sidelines, watching.

"What do I do?!" Scott cried. "What am I supposed to do?"

Dad cupped his hands and shouted. "Use the shield!"

"What?!"

"Just like we practiced!"

The faceless crushers kept roaring toward him, closer and closer.

"Use the shield!" Dad repeated.

"I don't know—*what shield?* What are you talking ab—"

Finally they hit him. Hard. Scott cried as they knocked the wind from him, as his head snapped back and he fell to the ground.

Suddenly he shot up in bed, wide-awake. He was breathing hard and covered in sweat. His eyes darted around the room as he fought to get his bearings.

Finally he took a deep breath and slowly

let it out. As he eased back onto the pillow, he tried to relax. But he knew sleep would be a long time returning. When he closed his eyes, all he saw were the shadowy giants. When he opened them, all he thought of was the Ouija board.

A half hour later, he was at his computer, entering the chat room. Lots of computer hackers were insomniacs. Somebody would be awake. Sure enough, in a moment a phrase appeared on his screen:

Welcome to Night Light
Name?
New Kid.
Password?
Dirty Socks

Immediately a menu appeared. He quickly scanned it until he found the topic entitled "Chat."

He moved his mouse down to the phrase and clicked it. Another phrase appeared.

Welcome to Night Light's Chat Line.

A pause followed. It was Scott's turn. Quickly he typed:

My name is New Kid. Is anybody out there?

A moment later, letters formed on his monitor.

Hello, New Kid . . .
Hi. We've just moved in. I go to Crescent Bay Jr. High. Who are you?

But instead of answering Scott's question, another question formed on the screen.

Isn't 3:37 A.M. a little late for a freshman to be up?

Scott wasn't fond of being lectured to, but he let it slide. He typed:

Tell me about it. I've been trying to sleep, but I've got a lot of junk on my mind.
Junk?
Yeah, you know—stuff. Listen, you don't happen to know anything about Ouija boards, do you?

Scott waited, but no words appeared on his screen. He typed again:

Hello, are you still there?

More silence. Again Scott typed:

Do you know anything about Ouija boards?

Finally the answer appeared on his screen. The words formed slowly, one letter at a time:

Be careful.

Once again, Scott felt the familiar chill creep across his back. He quickly typed:

Why? What do you mean?
Just . . . be careful, New Kid . . . be very careful.
What do you mean, be careful? Who are you?
My name is . . .

The letters hesitated, then continued:

Call me . . . Z. Good night.

"Wait a minute," Scott said as he quickly typed the words:

Please, don't hang up, not yet.
Z, are you there? Z? Z?

But Z had already disconnected.

Down the hall, Becka was having her own trouble sleeping. Granted, part of the problem was her skinned knees. Whenever she moved or dragged the blankets across them, they let her know how much they appreciated her little performance out on the track.

But that was small potatoes compared to what was going on in Becka's brain. It kept racing with thoughts of Julie, the amulet, and the Ascension Lady.

Should she warn Julie about the pouch or keep her mouth shut? After all, Becka was not like Scott. She couldn't make friends at the drop of a hat. It took time. The few friends she did make, she made for life. That's just how she was . . . faithful and giving to the end. But the initial work of making friends, that was always hard for her.

And now, out of the blue, one of the most popular girls in school was reaching out to her. If Becka tried to warn Julie this early in the relationship, she might ruin it. She might sound like some sort of superstitious fanatic. But if she didn't say something, what would happen to Julie?

She shook her head impatiently. What was she worried about? Nothing would happen. It was just a stupid little necklace.

But she'd seen too many things in Brazil . . . heard too many stories. Lots of the missionaries her dad had flown in and out of the jungle had tales about witch doctors and hexes and amulets and spirits . . . tales that made your hair stand on end and your blood run cold. Tales that they swore were true.

So the argument rolled around and around in her head. To tell or not to tell? Finally, she'd had enough. She threw off the covers, hopped out of bed, and padded downstairs to the kitchen for some munchies. Scott could have his fingernail chewing when things got tense; she preferred junk food.

She'd just shut the door of the fridge and started to unwrap last night's chicken when she heard it.

Scrape.

She froze. It was the same sound she'd heard in the garage the day before. Only now, in the stillness of the house, it seemed louder. She looked at the kitchen door leading to the garage. The sound stopped for a moment, then started . . . then stopped again.

Rebecca hesitated. A tiny knot formed in her stomach. She took a deep breath and forced it away. *Mom was right,* she thought, *it's probably just the wind.*

Or a giant rat . . .

Or a wild, vicious animal . . .

Or a ghastly ghoul hiding in the bizarre boxes at the back of the—

Stop it! Becka forced her mind to quit racing. Which almost worked until—

SCRAPE . . . SCRAPE.

She looked back to the door. What was she going to do—just stand there like some little kid afraid of the dark?

SCRAPE.

Somebody better check it out.

SCRAPE . . . SCRAPE.

And since there were no other volunteers, that somebody would have to be her. With another deep breath, Becka crossed to the door.

SCRAPE.

After a moment's hesitation and an extra breath just to be safe, she turned the knob and quickly threw open the door.

A light—a beam—streaked across the garage to the back wall of unopened boxes . . .

SCRAPE.

. . . and was gone.

Becka gasped. She fumbled for the switch. It took forever to find it and flood the garage with the much-welcomed light.

There was no movement. No sound. Everything was deathly silent.

Becka stood in the doorway, barely moving, barely breathing. That was definitely *not* the wind. And it definitely was not an animal. It was a light. But what kind of light shoots around garages in the middle of the night making strange noises?

Becka's heart pounded. She was frightened—really frightened—and she hated it. She hated being intimidated. She'd have to do something to get to the bottom of it . . . to prove it was all perfectly normal and explainable.

But not tonight. Not all alone. Not in her bare feet and sweats. Becka stepped back, snapped off the light, and closed the kitchen door.

Then, after a moment's hesitation, she reached down and locked it.

4

onday morning.

Scott knew he was in trouble the moment he entered the school. His first clue was the way a monster-sized kid, complete with skateboard tucked under his arm, picked him up and slammed him against his locker.

His second clue was the way the guy screamed into his face, "Mind your own business!"

But what really cinched it for Scott was when he couldn't lighten the mood with a joke. Humor was his speciality. That's how he stayed on everyone's good side. But before Scott could fire off some wisecrack about treating school property with respect or about not putting too many dents in the locker with the back of his head, Skateboard Kid threw open Scott's locker, tossed him inside, and slammed the door shut.

As the ringing in his ears faded, Scott could hear everyone outside laughing. No surprise there. After all, he was the new guy. Such things were expected. But he had no idea what Skateboard Kid had meant when he'd shouted . . . what was it? . . . "Mind your own business"?

Scott tried to relax. Other than the coat hook performing a little brain surgery in the back of his skull, things weren't too bad. Besides, if the Ouija board was right and he was going to die, it wouldn't be here. The way he figured, he was safer inside the locker with the coat hook than outside the locker in Skateboard Kid's hands. Eventually some teacher or janitor or vice principal would come to bail him out. Until then, he'd use the situation to his advantage. His humor shone best in tight situations, and it didn't get much tighter than in a locker. He began to whistle.

"What's that?" a voice asked.

"Listen," another said.

The hallway quieted down as Scott continued to whistle. It really wasn't a tune, just something he made up as he went along. But it did the trick.

He could hear the kids snickering. Then laughing.

Suddenly there was loud banging on the locker door. "Knock it off!" Skateboard Kid's voice shouted.

"Oh, sorry," Scott called. "I thought you were gone."

After a moment he began to sing:

"MINE EYES HAVE SEEN THE GLORY OF
THE COMING OF THE LORD.
HE IS TRAMPLING OUT THE VINTAGE
WHERE THE GRAPES OF WRATH ARE—"

BANG! BANG! BANG! "I said knock it off!"

"But I'm bored!"

More laughter outside.

Skateboard Kid's voice dripped with sarcasm. "I'm sorry if you find this an inconvenience. Perhaps I could get you something?"

So the big guy was trying to be clever. Great. That gave Scott home-court advan-

41

tage. "How 'bout a big-screen TV?" Scott quipped.

More laughter.

"Sorry, fresh out." It almost sounded like the guy was starting to have fun. He continued, "How 'bout a hot tub?"

"Nah," Scott shouted, "I left my shorts at home. But, hey, can I borrow your board? You know, work on some moves while I'm in here?"

More laughter, until the bell finally rang. The show was over. Scott could hear kids chuckling, talking, shuffling off. Unfortunately no one felt inclined to chuckle, talk, or shuffle off in his direction.

He continued to wait, trying to stay cool and calm. Nearly a minute passed before there was a quiet knock on the locker. "Scott, you there?" The squeaky question was followed by a loud sniff.

Darryl.

Scott sighed. "No, Scott stepped out for a bite to eat—but if you come back in about—"

"Stop fooling around," Darryl interrupted. "What's your combination?"

"32 . . ."

Scott could hear the combination dial spinning.

"25 . . ."

More spinning.

"12."

Suddenly the door opened and Scott stepped out—a little stiff from his cramped quarters, but still in one piece. "Thanks," he said, rubbing the coat-hanger dent from his neck.

"Don't mention it," Darryl said as he glanced around. "Don't mention it to anyone." He quickly turned and headed up the hall.

"Hey, wait up." Scott grabbed his first-period books and started after him.

But Darryl didn't slow.

"What's the hurry?" Scott asked as he caught up.

Darryl kept his fast pace. "You don't get it, do you?"

"Get what?"

"What just happened." They rounded the corner, and Darryl quickly searched the hall.

"Sure, I get it. I'm the new kid, which means I'm a walking target for low self-esteemed bullies from dysfunctional fami—"

"Stop joking," Darryl snapped.

"Who's joking?"

"It's nothing to laugh about."

"Lighten up." Scott tried to chuckle. "I'm the one who got thrown in the locker, remember? I'm the new kid who—"

"It has nothing to do with you being the new kid."

"Then what?"

Darryl's eyes kept combing the hall. "Listen, I gotta go," he squeaked. "And don't tell anyone I helped you."

"Darryl—"

Without another word, the little guy turned and darted into a classroom. Now Scott stood in the hallway all alone. Well, not quite all alone. Try as he might, he couldn't shake the feeling that, somehow, some way, he was being watched.

And, once again, that all-too-familiar chill started to move across his shoulders.

~

Things were almost as weird for Rebecca . . . but in the opposite way.

Scott was the star of the family, the life of the party. Oh sure, he was a little egotistical at times—what guy isn't?—but basically he was everyone's favorite. Becka, on the other hand, made it a point to stay in the background, generally doing her best imitation of a potted plant. She wasn't a geek or anything like that—she just tended to be quieter, more thoughtful . . . more boring.

But now . . .

"Hey, Krissi," Julie called across the cafeteria, "I want you to meet Becka."

Rebecca winced. Something about her name being shouted across the cafeteria made her uncomfortable. But she wasn't surprised. Ever since second period, Julie had made it her personal mission to introduce Becka to all her coolest and best friends. And since she was considered Julie's friend, that automatically made her their friend.

Of course, Rebecca knew it wouldn't last. As soon as they got to know her, they would drop her like a hot potato. But until then, there wasn't much she could do but play along.

"She's new," Julie continued as she plopped down at Krissi's table and motioned for Becka to do the same. "She's a great long-distance runner—going to help us beat Royal High in the Prelims next week."

Krissi flashed Becka a perfect smile, which was attached to a perfect face, which was attached to perfect hair, which was attached to—well, you probably get the picture.

Rebecca returned the smile and said nothing. She figured the longer she kept her mouth shut, the longer she could keep up the front.

"You're not the one who fell on her face Friday?" Krissi asked.

Becka's smile froze. So much for keeping up a front.

Immediately Julie came to the rescue. "She tripped over those stupid potholes. I keep telling Coach Simmons to fix them, but she keeps putting it off."

Krissi nodded and went back to eating.

Becka wasn't sure if Krissi had seen through her disguise or not. But she had no time to worry about it because suddenly there was another voice.

"Mind if we join you?"

Becka glanced up. An incredible-looking guy was grinning down at Krissi. And by "incredible," we're not talking your normal, everyday incredible. We're talking major "Did my heart just stop beating?" incredible. On the scale of one to ten, this guy was somewhere in the teens. Instinctively, Becka knew he was Krissi's boyfriend. He had to be. Who else would be dating this perfect Barbie but that perfect Ken?

"Hi, Philip," Krissi said, her face beaming as she scooted over to let the guy and his friend squeeze in.

Becka looked over to the friend and quickly sucked in her breath. It was the guy with the deep blue eyes.

"Hey, Becka." He flashed her a grin. "How you doing?"

Rebecca tried to smile. She wasn't sure if she succeeded. She wanted to answer, to say

something witty, but it's hard to be witty
when you can't find your voice.

"Ryan," Julie asked in surprise, "you two
know each other?"

"Sure do," Ryan said as he reached for the
salt. "We're old friends." He gave another
smile. "Right, Becka?"

Becka smiled back. She could feel her face
start to burn and her mouth go dry. She threw
another look to Julie, who was fiddling with
the pouch around her neck, sliding it back
and forth on its leather thong.

The pouch. Becka had almost forgotten.
But no matter how she tried, she couldn't
entirely put it out of her mind.

She glanced back to Ryan and froze. Her
eyes darted to the other kids . . . first Krissi,
then Philip. Suddenly she had no appetite.
But it wasn't because of Ryan's flirting or
Julie's friendliness. It wasn't even because
she was sitting with the coolest, most popular group in the cafeteria.

Becka could no longer eat because
around each of the kid's necks, she saw the
same, identical leather pouch that Julie wore.

~

It was a California scorcher. Ninety-five
point four degrees in the shade. A million
point seven degrees in the sun. No wind

from the ocean. No clouds in the sky. It was the type of day to skip class and hit the mall or to go to the beach. Definitely not the type of day for a P.E. class to be playing baseball outside.

Then again, P.E. was taught by Coach Dorsek, a man revered and hated by all. A man who, upon awakening that particular morning, discovered his entire front lawn had been t.p'd. A man who knew that if he made everyone suffer in every one of his P.E. classes, chances were he'd make the "more energy than they know what to do with" punks suffer, too.

The score was three to five. Scott's team trailed. So far our hero had grounded out, flown out, and struck out. The way he figured it, that was enough outs; now it was time to try for some hits. As he took the plate, a new pitcher was sent in. Maybe this was Scott's lucky break. Then again . . .

The first ball sizzled but was so far inside, Scott had to jump back to avoid getting hit. Some of the fourth-period lunch crowd who were watching from the stands whooped and hollered at the pitcher. But Scott turned back to him and grinned. No hard feelings. The kid was just warming up.

The second ball came in faster and even more inside. Scott hit the deck.

More whoops and hollers.

Scott rose and brushed himself off. This time he did not smile. Instead, he took his position as far back in the batter's box as possible—just to be safe.

Pitch three smoked across the outside corner for a strike.

Pitch four was a carbon copy.

Figuring the pitcher had finally found his groove, Scott stepped closer to the plate.

He didn't remember much after that. He didn't remember taking a couple of practice swings or the ball blazing toward him. And he didn't remember being hit so hard in the head that it cracked his batting helmet.

What he did remember was Coach Dorsek kneeling in front of him, holding out his fingers and yelling, "How many do you see?! How many do you see?!" He also remembered being lifted to his feet and carried toward the nurse's office.

And he remembered one other thing. He remembered the Ouija board's threat on his life.

~

By late afternoon, the sun had turned the track into a giant grill. Heat waves rippled and shimmered from its surface. And still the girls ran. They ran sprints; they ran 800s; they ran 1600s.

Julie had given Becka tips all afternoon. "Concentrate. Find your rhythm. Stay *focused*. That's the word. Count if you have to. One, two, one, two. But whatever you do, stay focused."

Now they were in their final lap of the mile, their last lap before hitting the showers. As usual, Julie had taken an early lead. That was her style. She never had a sprint to finish with, so she always took the lead early and kept far enough ahead to hold it—even against Becka's great end sprint.

But Becka was no threat to her—once again her mind was drifting. Once again it was back on Julie's pouch. Ever since lunch she'd fought with herself about talking to Julie. Shoot, she'd even practiced what to say. But no matter how she worded it, she still sounded like some superstitious old fogey.

For example, there was, "Excuse me, did you know that necklace of yours—the one that Ascension Lady gave you—is totally evil and straight from the devil?"

Then, of course, there was the more subtle approach. "I just love your jewelry. Oh, by the way, do you know it's used by witch doctors in demonic rituals?"

Any way she worded it, Becka would

sound like a fool. What was worse, she could kiss her popularity with the in crowd good-bye—which explained why she didn't say a word. She just kept her mouth shut. And the civil war kept raging inside her head:

Julie's your friend. She deserves to be warned.

You're absolutely right, Becka agreed with herself.

But you didn't make her wear it. Don't you deserve a little popularity?

You're absolutely right, Becka agreed again.

But what about Julie?

And so the debate continued, spinning around in her head until, to her surprise, Becka noticed she had somehow stumbled across the finish line. It wasn't a pretty sight as she tripped and practically fell, but at least she'd made it.

She came to a stop a few feet from Julie. They both leaned over trying to catch their breath. Julie spoke first. "Becka, you gotta concentrate; you gotta stay focused."

Becka nodded, unable to speak.

Julie coughed, then took another gulp of air. "You can beat Royal. We both can."

Again Becka nodded.

"Numero Uno, just you and me . . . but you've gotta stay focused."

"All right," Becka finally croaked. "I hear you, I hear you."

Julie cracked a smile. "Just being a friend, kiddo."

Becka glanced up and tried to return the smile. But she couldn't. All she could think was, *Shouldn't I do the same? Shouldn't I be a friend?*

5

hat baseball
hit you too hard on the noggin."

"No, Beck, I'm serious." Scott slumped in
the chair in front of his computer. His head
still hurt from his little "who turned out the
lights" routine in P.E. But after a trip to the
nurse's office, then some X rays over at the
hospital ER, they found nothing broken.

"Maybe a little scrambled," the doctor teased, "but nothing broken."

Immediately Cornelius hopped off the desk and crawled up Scott's arm, chattering, "E. T. PHONE HOME. *SQUAWK!* PHONE HOME, PHONE HOME!"

Scott absentmindedly handed him a section of orange. Cornelius stopped talking and gratefully devoured it. Scott looked at his sister. "I really think there's someone— or some*thing*—out to get me."

"Puh-leeese . . . ," Becka said scornfully. "Why? Just 'cause once in your life you're not Mr. Popularity?"

He shook his head. "C'mon Beck, you know me better than that."

Becka sighed. She did know him better than that. In fact, she knew him better than anyone. And he knew her, too. They'd never admit it, but whether they liked it or not, the two were each other's best friend. Maybe it had something to do with being the only American kids living in the Brazilian rain forest . . . or having to constantly make new friends as their parents kept moving from town to town.

Or maybe it was losing Dad.

Whatever the reason, on average days they fought like cats and dogs. But whenever the chips were down, like now, they were always there for each other.

Becka leaned against Scott's dresser and gave a quick recap. "So you go into some bookstore, interrupt a bunch of kids playing some game that makes a stupid threat, and now you think something's out to get you?"

"It was more than just a bookstore," Scott insisted.

"What do you mean?"

"Do you remember Takuma, the old witch doctor? Remember how creepy we'd feel whenever we got near his place?"

"With all his charms and the demonic junk inside?"

Scott nodded. "Well, that's the kind of stuff I saw in the Bookshop, and that's exactly how I felt when I walked inside."

"Hold it; wait a minute." Rebecca felt a twinge of uneasiness. "There were, like, occult things inside there?"

Again Scott nodded. "I didn't recognize a lot of 'em, but—"

"What about charms?"

He looked at her.

"You know, leather pouches with stuff inside, like Takuma would make for the villagers."

Scott shrugged. "I suppose. That kind of stuff, yeah."

Rebecca slowly sat on his bed.

"You OK?"

"This bookstore. . . ," she said slowly. "What was its name?"

"Why? What's—"

"Just . . ." She cut him off, then drew a slow breath. "Do you remember the name?"

"They called it 'The Ascension Bookshop,' whatever that means."

Becka knew exactly what it meant. She took a deep breath. *The Ascension Lady . . .* that was what Julie called the woman who made her the pouch. But it wasn't her name; it was where she worked. The Ascension Lady—just like they'd call a woman who worked at a drugstore the drugstore lady, or a bank clerk the bank lady.

"Beck, you OK? Rebecca?"

Was it possible? Was there actually a place like Takuma's where kids were given demonic charms? A place right here in Crescent Bay where kids hung out and practiced . . . practiced . . . ?

Suddenly Becka turned to Scott. "What about this game they were playing?"

"It was more than a game. They took it pretty serious. Darryl called it a 'Ouija board.' You ever hear of it?"

Becka hadn't, but having lived in the jungles of Brazil, there were lots of things she'd never heard of. "And you think there was something wrong about it?" she asked.

Scott nodded as he turned to boot up the computer. "Not just me. Take a look." He typed a few strokes and clicked the mouse a couple times to bring Z's warning back onto the screen.

But nothing appeared.

"That's funny," Scott said, hitting a few more keys and moving the mouse. "I thought for sure I saved it."

Again the screen came up blank.

"What are you looking for?"

Without a word, Scott entered the Night Light chat room. "There's this guy, Z—I talked to him Saturday night and—" He broke off, peering at the screen. "Hey, check it out."

Rebecca rose to her feet and looked over Scott's shoulder. He had just typed in his password, and now the screen read:

Hello New Kid, you have a message.
Read now? Y OR N.
Y.

Immediately the screen cleared and his message came up:

To: New Kid
From: Z
Topic: Ouija Boards

"That's him," Scott said, pointing to the screen. "That's the guy I was telling you about." With a click of the mouse, Scott paged down. The screen read:

After our little talk I did some research.
Please read carefully. I will have more soon.
AGE: Ouija boards have been used in one form or another since about 600 B.C.
PURPOSE: To communicate with the dead.

Scott and Rebecca exchanged glances. Scott paged down to the next screen:

TODAY'S USE: Today's version is treated as a toy and sold in many department stores. It is a flat, smooth board with letters and numbers on it. A pointer moves under the hand of the "players" and spells out answers to questions asked.

"That's it," Scott exclaimed. "That's exactly what they were doing."
"Shhh." Becka scowled. They read on:

DOES IT WORK?: Many "occult experiences" can be faked or subconsciously controlled by the subject. The same is true with Ouija boards. But that is not always the case. Often the messages given by the board go beyond what the players know.

Scott hesitated, then paged down to the next screen:

Numerous tests have been performed where the players have been blindfolded and the board's alphabet rearranged. It still worked with such speed and accuracy that the only answer is "supernatural intervention."

Scott leaned back in his chair and took a deep breath. "What's all that mean?"

Rebecca frowned. "If that board's really working, and the kids aren't moving it themselves . . ." She paused, looking at Scott, her eyes serious. "It means we're dealing with spirits."

Scott's eyes widened. "You mean like demons?"

Rebecca bit her lip and slowly nodded. "Yes . . . demons."

6

The following morning, Becka stumbled down the stairs to join her family at the breakfast table.

"Hey, Buckwheat," Scott called, between stuffing his face with spoonfuls of Kix. "What'll it be—Kix without milk or . . . no milk with Kix?"

Becka scowled at him through puffy eyes.

She definitely was not a morning person. Unfortunately, Scott was. And for some reason, he seemed to think it was his personal mission to make sure everyone was as cheery as he was.

"I'm sorry," Mom said, referring to the lack of milk. "I promise as soon as things settle down and I get a job, we'll get back to normal."

"Any leads yet?" Scott asked.

"A couple," Mom said, grabbing some juice from the fridge and pouring it. "Should know in a day or so."

Once again Becka felt a sadness creep over her. Mom always worked so hard to keep everyone happy. Even when Dad had died, she'd spent more time making sure the kids were OK than she ever spent on herself. Sometimes Becka marveled at Mom's strength and ability to give. Other times it made her feel sad and even a little guilty.

"Did either of you leave that door open last night?" Mom asked, motioning toward the kitchen door leading to the garage.

Scott and Rebecca both shook their heads.

"That's funny. I came down about 1:30 last night, and it was standing wide open."

Becka's eyes shot to the door.

"And there was this strange sound," Mom said, glancing to her daughter. "Kind of like you described when we were moving the boxes."

Becka froze. She threw a look to Scott, but he was too busy eating to notice. She cleared her throat and tried her best to sound casual. "Did you see anything?"

"Well, no," Mom answered. "Not that I really tried. I just sort of shut the door, locked it, and ran for my life." She chuckled, a little embarrassed.

Scott gave a snort.

Becka said nothing. Mom had enough worries. She didn't need any more. But Becka's mind was racing again, trying to piece it all together: the amulet, the Ascension Lady, the attacks against Scott . . . the demons.

And now this. A door that she definitely had locked, that was now unlocked and standing wide open.

Was there a connection between all these things? Probably not. But still . . . She gave another look at the door. It was shut and securely locked. And that was good enough for now.

At least, she hoped so.

∿

"Excuse me. . . . Sorry. . . . Excuse me. . . ." Scott continued climbing up the bleachers, stepping on more than one pair of feet.

"Hey, watch it, Hairball!" It was Skate-board Kid.

"Hey, how you doing?" Scott said, then continued on, "Excuse me. . . . Pardon me. . . . Sorry. . . ."

He had tried to talk to Darryl all morning, but the little guy would have nothing to do with him. Every time he saw Scott coming from one direction, he'd head the other.

Until now.

Now they were all taking their seats for some sort of assembly—an antidrugs or "crime don't pay 'cause prison's the pits" talk. Every school has them, where some guy comes in and rambles on about messing up his life because he did what he did and how you should never do it because if you do, you'll mess up your life just like he did. At any rate, everyone was gathered to listen.

After crawling over a few dozen more people and toes . . .

"OUCH!"

"Sorry."

"Watch it!"

Scott finally managed to squeeze in next to Darryl.

"What are you doing here?" Darryl squeaked. His eyes darted around nervously.

"We've got to talk," Scott answered.

"Not here, not in the open."

"You've been avoiding me all day."

Before they could continue, Principal Slayter had everyone stand for the flag salute. Next he introduced their guest speaker, Assistant Police Chief somebody-or-other. He was a heavy man with a great sense of humor, but Scott and Darryl weren't laughing. The reason was simple. They weren't listening.

"All I'm saying," Scott whispered, "is if those kids aren't moving that Ouija board pointer by themselves, then something else is moving it."

"Duh." Darryl said sarcastically. "Of course something is moving it. Spirits."

Scott was stunned. "You mean you know about them?"

"Of course."

"And you—you actually fool around with them?"

"That's the whole point, brainless. We call up the spirits of the dead and ask them all sorts of—"

"The dead?" Scott interrupted so loudly that Mrs. Pederson, a teacher four rows down, turned around and scowled. Scott gave an apologetic nod, then continued more softly. "Those aren't spirits of dead people, Darryl."

"What are they then?"

"Demons."

"Demons?!" Darryl half cried, half squeaked.

Again Mrs. Pederson turned and glared.

Again the boys looked to her apologetically. This time there were also a few snickers from nearby students.

The two guys looked ahead, pretending to be interested in the assistant chief's speech—something about locking up your bicycles—but they could only fake it for a few moments.

Soon Darryl was leaning back over to Scott and whispering, "They can't be demons."

"Why not?"

"Because they say they're dead people. They give us their names."

"They're lying."

"How do you know?" Darryl asked.

"The dead can't come back and talk to us. It's impossible."

"Who says?"

"The Bible."

"THE BIBLE?!"

This time Darryl was so loud that the assistant police chief stopped and looked toward their section. "I'm sorry, was there a question?"

More kids chuckled. But not Mrs. Pederson.

"No, Chief," she said, rising to her feet. "Just a couple of rather ill-mannered children. I do apologize." She turned to Scott and Darryl and motioned for them to join her.

There were plenty more snickers as Scott and Darryl got up and headed down the bleachers to join Mrs. Pederson. Without a word, she escorted them toward the door. Of course the assistant chief resumed his speech, but of course everyone was too busy shaking their heads and chuckling to hear what he said.

~

"What do you mean, 'evil'?" Julie grinned.

Rebecca didn't grin back.

"You're not serious are you?" Julie asked.

Becka swallowed hard and gave half a shrug. All day she'd tried to work up the courage to tell Julie about the amulet. Now, as they headed down the hall toward the locker room and practice, it seemed as good a time as any. There weren't too many people around, so if she made a fool of herself, it would at least be in private and not—

"Hey, Krissi!" Julie called across the hall. "Listen to this."

So much for privacy.

"Yeah? What's up?" Krissi asked, joining them.

"Becka here's got something to tell you."

Once again Becka took a deep breath.

The girls waited.

Finally she started, "It's just that those, uh, those charms you're wearing—"

"She's talking about our lucky pouches," Julie interrupted. "She says they're evil. Satanic."

It was Krissi's turn to grin.

Becka looked to the floor. Her face grew hot.

"I don't know about 'evil,'" Krissi said brightly, "but they're definitely satanic. Sure."

Becka snapped her head back up in surprise.

Krissi continued to smile. "Oh, don't worry, not satanic like the mean ol' devil with a pitchfork. But satanic like they're supposed to unlock the deeper forces of nature or something like that. At least, that's what Priscilla says."

"Priscilla?" Becka asked.

"Yeah," Julie answered, "the Ascension Lady who makes this stuff."

"The lady at the Bookshop?" Becka asked.

"Yeah." Krissi nodded. "She says she's a witch. But a good witch—you know, someone who uses the forces for good. Hey, I gotta go. Philip's going to surprise me with this incredible earring, with a diamond and everything."

"If it's a surprise, how do you know what it is?" Julie asked.

"I'm a professional hint dropper." Krissi laughed as she turned and headed back up the hall.

Julie shook her head in amusement until she saw the concerned look on Becka's face. "Lighten up," she said as she pushed open the locker-room door. "Krissi's an airhead, you know that. Nobody believes in witches and that junk. My pouch is just a lucky charm, like a rabbit's foot."

Becka opened her mouth but couldn't find the words.

~

Detention wasn't as bad as Scott feared. Nothing like in the movies, where the hero sits next to the all-school bully who's just waiting to turn his face into pizza topping.

Nope. Detention was just Scott and Darryl sitting in the library for one hour after school. And Mr. Lowry, the librarian, was so cool he didn't even care if they talked, as long as they kept it down.

"So what makes you an expert in all this spirit stuff?" Darryl asked, sniffing and pushing up his glasses.

"We lived down in South America," Scott bragged. Pride wasn't a huge problem with him . . . just big enough. "Yeah, we had to deal with the occult lots of times."

"Occult?"

"You know, demons, Satan—that kind of garbage."

"Did weird stuff ever happen?"

"Oh sure." Scott pretended to yawn. "We had to deal with this stuff all the time." A definite exaggeration—he'd only heard the stories from missionaries and his dad; he hadn't actually seen anything for himself. Even so, Scott's words did the trick. Darryl's eyes grew as big as saucers.

"Weren't you ever, you know . . . scared?"

"Nah . . ." By now Scott had crossed the line from exaggeration to lying, so he tried to pull it back a little. "Actually," he cleared his throat, "Mom and Dad, they were the ones who usually handled it when things happened." He noticed a trace of disappointment crossing Darryl's face, so he quickly threw in, "But the Bible says any Christian can beat that stuff."

"Yeah?"

Scott nodded. "Jesus gave us authority over Satan and all the demons." He was still bragging, but at least this part was the truth.

"So. . . ," Darryl mumbled, mostly to himself, "that's why they're doing it."

"'Who's 'they'?" Scott asked. "Doing what?"

"Huh?" Darryl glanced up. He looked a little sheepish. "Nothing, I just, uh—"

"Who are you talking about?" Scott held his eyes.

"No one, I—"

"Come on, Darryl. Who's doing what? What's going on?"

Darryl faltered. Scott pressed in, refusing to back down. "You know, don't you? You know what's going on."

Darryl looked down at the table and finally nodded.

Scott waited.

"It's the Society. They said the spirits or demons or whatever told them to hassle you."

"Why?"

Darryl shrugged. "I guess 'cause they're afraid of you."

"The demons?" Scott asked, a little surprised.

Again Darryl nodded.

The pieces slowly started to fit together. "So it's . . ." Scott hesitated.

Darryl finished his thought. "It's the Society that's doing all the stuff to you, yeah."

"Not the Ouija board . . . or something weird?"

Darryl nodded. "The way I hear it, the pitcher that beaned you yesterday is about twenty bucks richer."

Scott listened on. Part of him was relieved—no one likes to think there are spirits out to get him—but part of him was also growing angry.

Darryl continued. "They wanted to scare you, to make sure you wouldn't come back."

"No problem there," Scott said quietly.

"Yeah, but . . ."

Scott looked up.

Darryl was doing his own bit of thinking. "If you're so much stronger, if you're that much of a threat—I mean, you could go in there and really show 'em your stuff, couldn't you?"

Scott was flattered and cautious at the same time. "Well, I uh . . . I don't think—"

"OK, guys." It was Mr. Lowry. "Your time's up. You're free to go home."

The boys looked at the clock in surprise. It was the fastest hour they'd ever spent.

"I trust you'll be a little more courteous the next time we have guests," he said.

The kids nodded as they gathered their stuff and headed toward the door. But the conversation wasn't over.

"The way I see it," Darryl gave another sniff, "either you're stronger than these demon guys or you're not."

"No question," Scott insisted. "Jesus said he gave us power and authority over all—"

"Then you need to prove it."

"What do you mean, 'prove it'?"

Darryl shoved open the library door, and they stepped into the hall. "Either Jesus is lying when he says you're stronger, or he's telling the truth. The only way to know for certain is by going back to the Society and proving it."

"Darryl, I don't think that's—"

"What's the matter? You're not chicken, are you?"

Scott bristled at the word. "No! It's not that. . . ." His mind raced, wondering how he got himself into this predicament and, more important, how he'd get himself out.

"Then I'll tell the rest of the kids, and we'll see if they want a showdown." Darryl nodded to himself as if the decision was made. He pushed open the outside doors, and they stepped into the late afternoon sun.

"Darryl," Scott said, "I don't think that's such a good—"

"It should be cool," Darryl interrupted. "Everybody will be there."

Before Scott could protest, a horn honked.

73

"That's my mom." Darryl said as he turned and started toward an approaching van. "I'll let you know what's happening as soon as I hear anything."

"Darryl, I don't think . . ."

But Darryl wasn't listening.

"Darryl? . . . Darryl!"

Darryl opened the van door, and immediately his mom began yelling at him for getting into trouble. He gave Scott a roll of the eyes—parents, sheesh!—and slammed the door.

Scott stared after the van as it sped off. Then he glanced down to his fingernails. He was gnawing on them again.

∿

"You shot off your big mouth again, didn't you, Scotty."

"Beck—"

"Some day that pride of yours is really going to get you in hot water."

"I think I'm already there."

Rebecca sank down on his bed. Cornelius hopped off his perch and started walking up her leg. "Doesn't the Bible say we're not supposed to test God and stuff?" she asked.

"Nobody's testing God," Scott said with a sigh. He snapped on the computer and

74

typed in Night Light's number to see if he had any messages. "But somebody's got to prove to those morons who's the strongest."

"And that somebody's going to be you."

Scott shrugged.

Rebecca rolled onto her back and stared at the ceiling. "Why wasn't I an only child?" she moaned.

"Hey, check it out," Scott said. "I got another message from Z." He brought it up onto the screen.

With the slightest sigh Becka sat up and read over Scott's shoulder:

To New Kid:
Another way of proving supernatural contact through the Ouija board is in the number of possession cases. Here's the rest of the information I promised: "Psychics and parapsychologists have received letters from hundreds of people who have experienced 'possession' (an invasion of their personalities). Rev. Donald Page, a well-known clairvoyant and exorcist of the Christian Spiritualist Church, is reported as saying that most of his 'possession' cases 'are people who have used the Ouija board,' and that 'this is one of the easiest and quickest ways to become possessed.'"

New Kid, when a person is "possessed," a demon has come inside a person and is controlling him or her. I warn you, this is not something to play with. Exercise extreme caution.

Z

Scott let out a low whistle, and he and Becka exchanged looks.

"He's right, Scotty, this is serious stuff."

"I know," Scott said with a heavy sigh. "But Christians still have the power, right? I mean, I can still show them who's boss."

Rebecca looked to her little brother. Once again, she wasn't sure what to say. All she was sure of was the uneasiness she felt growing inside.

7

hey hit you
pretty hard, didn't they, Son?"

It was another dream. Scott lay flat on his
back in the middle of the football field. His
dad was still in his suit of armor as he
offered him his hand. Scott took it and
slowly rose to his feet.

He knew he was dreaming, but with all

this talk of spirits and demons and communicating with the dead, he still had to be sure. "You're not really my dad, are you?"

The man burst out laughing. "Of course not, Scotty. I'm a memory of your dad. Your dad's in heaven with the Lord. You know that."

Scott nodded.

"I'm just your imagination trying to get you to remember something."

"Well, for an imagination, you look pretty real."

"Thanks." The man smiled, wiping a smudge off his metal breastplate. "Now tell me, why didn't you use your shield? Or run one of our plays?"

"I don't . . . I don't remember any plays." Scott sighed.

"Of course you remember." His dad chuckled. "We read from the Playbook every day."

Scott stared. "What plays are you talking about? What playbook?"

"The one your mother and I read to you and Becka at the breakfast table."

"We never read any playbook at any breakfast—"

"Sure we did."

"Dad, the only thing we ever read at the table was—" Suddenly Scott stopped. Wait a minute! They did read something at the

table. Nearly every day. But it wasn't a football playbook.

Scott looked at his father. "Are you talking
about the Bible? Is that what you're trying to
get me to remember?"

The man grinned. "Bingo. Now, we
haven't got much time, so let's get back in
there."

They turned and started toward the line
of scrimmage. Once again it was the two of
them against an entire squad of shadowy
giants. But as Scott looked up, the shadows
suddenly disappeared. Now he clearly saw
their faces—they were the kids from the Society! The chubby brunette in black, the red-
haired beauty, and the meaty guy in the tank
top. They were all there in front of him.
They were bigger—much, *much* bigger—but
it was definitely them.

Scott's mind spun as he tried to figure out
what was going on. Sure, their family read
the Bible, but what did that have to do with
football? Or with these kids who were loom-
ing over him like overfed gorillas . . . gorillas
waiting to turn him into human hamburger?

Dad took his position over the ball and
waited for Scott's signal.

The Society dug in their cleats, waiting to
make the kill.

Scott took a deep breath. *Oh well,* he

thought, *it's only a dream, right?* He crouched behind his dad and yelled. "Ready! . . . Set! . . . HIKE!

Dad snapped the ball. But it wasn't a ball. It wasn't a shield, either. Not this time. This time Scott was holding a sword. A sword with all sorts of words and letters on it.

The Society sprung toward him grunting and growling.

"Remember the Playbook!" Dad shouted. "Use your sword! Use your sword!"

Scott dropped back. The Society giants thundered toward him.

"Remember the playbook! Use your sword!"

Scott was at a loss. He had no idea what to do.

The meaty guy was the first to hit him, knocking out all his wind.

"OOAAFF!" Scott gasped.

The others followed, one after another, leaping on top of him, stomping him . . . crushing him.

Scott screamed, but nobody heard. Nobody cared. There was only his pain and the Society as they continued piling on top of him, one after another, grinding his body into the mud.

"Aughh!" he screamed again. "AUGHHHHHHHHH!"

"Scotty! Scotty, wake up." It was Mom. What was she doing on the field?

"Scotty, you're having a nightmare. Scott, wake up, wake up!"

Scott's eyes fluttered open. He was sweating and gasping, but at least the pain was gone and he was back in his room. At least he was no longer football road kill.

His mom was on the edge of his bed, holding his shoulders tightly, her eyes filled with concern. "Are you all right?" she asked gently. "I heard you screaming."

"Yeah," Scott said, trying to catch his breath. "I think so. I just . . . it was a dream . . . about Dad . . ." His voice trailed off, and when tears jumped to his eyes, he was too tired to hold them back.

His mom pulled him close and held him. "I know, Scotty," she said. "I know. I miss him, too."

Scott wasn't sure how long they sat holding each other. But he didn't care. All he knew was that he needed it.

They both did.

∿

The next morning, Scott was still trying to figure out the dream as he stood at his locker, dialing the combination.

"It's all set," Darryl's voice squeaked.

"What?" Scott glanced up. "Oh, hi, Darryl."

"The Society has agreed to meet you at the Bookshop after school."

"Today?"

"Of course today. You are ready, right?"

"Listen, Darryl, I don't—"

"You're not chickening out?"

"No, it's not that. It's—"

"Good. Cause they said you would. They said—"

"Hold it," Scott interrupted. "They said I'd chicken out?"

"Sure. They said you'd be afraid to take them on." Darryl gave a louder than normal sniff.

Scott could feel himself getting angry. Before he knew it, he shot back, "You tell them I'm not afraid of anybody." He slammed the locker shut. "You tell them I'll be there." With that, he turned and stormed off.

"Great!" Darryl called after him. "It's gonna be great!"

Scott slowly let out his breath. He wished he could agree. But he was already feeling lousy. Why couldn't he keep his big mouth shut?

~

"Let me get this straight," Krissi said, almost letting a frown wrinkle the perfect skin of her perfect forehead. "You're saying if we keep wearing these things, we're all going to become like the girl in *The Exorcist?*"

Julie and the other kids at the lunch table snickered. Once again Julie had brought the subject up, and once again Becka was having to defend herself. "All I'm saying is that some witch doctors use those charms to control other people."

"What exactly do you mean by 'control'?" Ryan asked. His blue eyes looked at her intently. Becka was grateful that at least one person seemed to be taking her seriously.

"She means like demon possession," Philip explained.

Becka shook her head. "Not really. It's just a way witch doctors get people to depend on their charms instead of themselves . . . or God."

"You like really know witch doctors?" Krissi asked.

"Wow!" Julie exclaimed.

Rebecca could tell they were getting off the subject. But before she could get them back on, she noticed Philip. His body was going rigid. He was becoming as stiff as a board.

Julie laughed and slapped him on the arm. "Knock it off, Philip."

But Philip didn't respond. For a moment, there was a look of panic on his face . . .

then it went totally blank. His eyes rolled up into his head, and he started choking.

"Philip. . . ," Krissi scolded. She was certain he was clowning. Well, almost certain.

But as the choking continued, Becka thought he might be having some sort of seizure. Maybe it was epilepsy or . . .

She tried to push back the thought.

. . . something worse.

"Philip." Krissi was louder now. And frightened. "That's not very funny. Philip!"

The choking increased until it sounded inhuman—like some monster or alien. The kids from the surrounding tables stopped their conversations and turned to stare.

"Philip! Knock it off! Philip?!"

Ryan snickered. He still didn't believe it was true. But then Philip spoke. Well, at least Philip's mouth spoke. His voice was different. Deeper. Sinister.

"Philip is no longer here—we have control now."

"Philip?" Krissi shook him, but he didn't react. "Philip, answer me!" Her voice grew louder. "What do you want with him? Who are you?"

"Our needs are simple."

"Who are you? Where's Philip?"

"Our needs are simple," the voice repeated.

"What do you want?!"

"Pass the salt, please—this hamburger casserole is gross."

There was a moment of stunned silence, then everyone broke into laughter. Philip, Ryan, Julie—everybody roared. Well, almost everybody. Krissi was too busy giving Philip a punch to the arm.

Then there was Becka. "Excuse me," she mumbled hoarsely as she rose and quickly dashed from the table.

"Becka," Ryan called. "Hey, Becka, it was just a joke. Come on back. . . ."

But Rebecca wasn't coming back. She wasn't mad. She just didn't want them to see the tears filling her eyes.

~

As they approached the Bookshop, Scott was nervous. Actually, scared spitless.

But not for long . . .

The handsome, middle-aged woman was no longer there. She had been replaced by some pimply-faced, high school kid.

"Where's Priscilla?" Darryl asked.

"She, uh . . . she said she had some errands to run. She'll be back after the, uh . . ." He motioned to Scott. "You know, after you guys are through."

"She didn't want to be here?" Darryl

squeaked in surprise. "She didn't want to see the fireworks?"

The guy shrugged. "I'm just telling you what she said."

"Cool." Darryl gave a loud sniff as they passed the counter and headed down the hall.

"What's cool?" Scott asked.

"She doesn't want to meet you."

"Who?"

"Priscilla, the lady who runs this place."

"Why not?"

"Sounds like she might be afraid."

"Yeah?" Scott could feel a twinge of the ol' pride returning.

Darryl sniffed again. "Maybe you have too much power for her to handle."

Suddenly Scott was feeling more confident. Somehow he seemed to be standing just a little bit taller, his chest swelling just a little bit bigger. Who knew—maybe he'd call fire down out of the sky to burn up the Ouija board (he'd read something like that in the Bible). Or maybe he'd make the kids unable to speak until they acknowledged God's power (he'd read that, too). He wasn't sure. But whatever he did, it would be awesome.

They arrived at the door. It was closed.

Darryl turned to him and pushed up his glasses. "You sure you're ready?"

Scott nodded. "Let's do it."

Darryl sniffed and slowly opened the door.

Once again the room was dark, except for the dozen or so candles flickering. Once again the kids looked up—the chubby brunette in black, the pretty redhead, and the meaty guy. There were plenty of other kids sitting around, too. More than Scott remembered from the last time. But that was OK. Obviously they wanted to see the show.

"Come on in," Meaty Guy said, trying to sound casual. (He might have pulled it off if it wasn't for the way his voice quivered.)

Scott smiled. He strode confidently into the room, and for good reason: The Ascension Lady had run off, the kids were shaking in their boots, and he, Scott Williams, had the power of God behind him. Not a bad combination.

This was going to be a piece of cake.

8

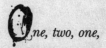ne, two, one, two, one, two . . .

One lap to go. Becka counted, she concentrated, she did everything Julie taught her. Everything to keep focused on the 1600 they were completing.

The Prelims were tomorrow. She and Julie would run the mile, the half mile, and probably a couple of the longer sprints. Who knows, if she did well, she might even help Julie beat Royal High.

But that wasn't the real reason she ran. Becka ran to forget the afternoon. She ran to forget the laughter, the snickers, the put-downs.

Ever since Philip's little possession routine at the lunch table, word had spread. Suddenly everyone knew her as the "Church Lady"—the superstitious Christian who believed the devil lurked behind every shadow.

One, two, one, two . . .

Julie ran half a dozen steps ahead. As usual, her rhythms were smooth and flowing. It infuriated Becka. Not Julie's running, but that Julie hadn't stood up for her. In fact, Julie was the one who had started it. And she was still spreading it . . . and enjoying it!

One, two, one, two, one, two . . .

Once again Becka's lungs were on fire, but that was nothing compared to the anger smoldering in her heart. This was her reward for trying to help Julie? For trying to warn her? Total humiliation!

Half a lap to go.

What did Julie think? That because Becka was quiet, she didn't have feelings? That because they were friends, she could get away with that kind of junk?

She looked ahead to Julie. Miss Perfect, Miss "I've got the great looks and money and friends." Who did she think she was, anyway?

Becka's anger continued to burn—until an idea took root. She never thought she'd be able to take Julie. Julie was the expert, the teacher, the one destined to go to State. But there she was, not that far away . . . and with no sprint to rely on for the end.

A strength surged through Rebecca—a strength connected with her anger. It started somewhere in her chest and flowed into her arms and legs. Her energy increased more than ever before. With two hundred meters to go, it was too soon to begin her sprint— way too soon. But it didn't matter. She started to count faster.

One, two, one, two, one, two . . .

She began closing the gap.

Coach Simmons was the first to spot it. "What's Becka doing?"

Others looked up and watched. Becka continued to count, to dig in.

One hundred meters to go.

A couple of kids started to shout, to cheer her on. "All right, Becka! Go for it!"

One two one two one two . . .

91

Inch by inch, she moved up until she finally pulled beside Julie. The look of astonishment on the girl's face almost brought enough satisfaction to Becka. Almost.

Who *did* she think she was, anyway?

Becka pushed harder.

Julie panicked. For a moment she lost her rhythm.

Perfect. Rebecca inched ahead.

Fifty meters to go.

Now it was an all-out race. Just the two of them. Becka was beyond exhaustion. Her lungs ached, but her rage was stronger than her pain.

One two one two one two . . .

Julie tried to keep up, but she had no sprint. She fell two strides behind, then three. Once again Becka heard the girl break her rhythm, but she didn't look back. She didn't have to.

Twenty meters.

"Atta girl, Becka!" kids shouted. "Kick it in, girl, kick it in!"

OneTwoOneTwoOneTwo . . .

Ten meters.

She could almost hear Julie's heart breaking.

Good.

Five meters.

Becka stretched and crossed the line—six strides ahead of Julie. She stumbled and practically fell as she came to a stop, but the team members were there to catch her and congratulate her.

"Way to go girl! 5:51!" Coach Simmons shouted. "That was incredible! You, too, Julie." She turned to Julie who was standing behind her. "5:53! Your best time ever! You girls are going to stomp Royal tomorrow!"

Becka stayed hunched over, gulping air. She could hear Julie coughing and gasping beside her. But she didn't look. Instead, she rose, turned, and started for the showers.

A couple more kids congratulated her, but Becka paid little attention. She had won. She had beaten Julie, and that was all that counted.

"Hey Becka . . . Becka!" It was Julie's voice. But Becka ignored her as she continued toward the showers. Revenge was sweet. More than sweet. It was glorious.

And if she could do it today, she could do it tomorrow!

∾

Back at the Bookshop, Meaty Guy continued with the opening remarks. "So how do you want to do this?"

Scott shrugged. "It's your show."

The redhead stepped forward. "My name's Kara. This is James." She motioned to Meaty Guy. "And Brooke, here, she's our president."

The girl in black nodded. She was obviously the coolest and most collected of the group. At least that's how she looked on the outside. On the inside, Scott figured she was shaking like the others.

He approached the Ouija board, trying his best to appear calm. And why not? After all, he was holding all the cards. He glanced around the room, peering into the darkness. Then, motioning to the candles, he quipped, "So what's the deal? You guys forget to pay the electrical bill?"

No one laughed. Not even a smile. So they wanted to play hardball, did they? Fine. He could do that.

Brooke spoke next. "Darryl here says you think the Society is a hoax, that we have no power."

"Not exactly," Scott corrected. "I believe there's power here . . . just the wrong type."

Brooke looked on, waiting.

Scott motioned to the Ouija board's pointer. "If you guys aren't moving that thing around, then something else is. And that something else is definitely unfriendly."

A brief silence hung over the room until Brooke finally answered. "Granted . . . sometimes we wake a rather cranky spirit from the dead, but—"

"No way," Scott broke in. She glared at him over the interruption, but he continued. "Those aren't spirits of the dead you're talking to."

"If they're not spirits of the dead," she asked, "then who are they?"

Scott shrugged. "Just your average, run-of-the-mill demons."

"And by demons you mean . . . ?"

"The bad guys. The angels that got kicked out of heaven with Satan."

Brooke looked at him a moment. "Interesting," was all she said.

"Truth," was all he said.

After another pause, she continued. "Yes, well, we'll see, won't we?" With that she placed her fingertips on the plastic pointer and nodded to Meaty Guy to do the same. There was a slight shuffling in the room as the kids moved in for a better view.

Brooke threw back her head and closed her eyes. "So tell me," she said, still speaking to Scott, "who would you like to talk to?"

"Got me," Scott forced a grin. "How 'bout Fred Flintstone."

A couple kids chuckled.

"Get real," Meaty Guy scowled. "It has to be somebody dead. You know, like—"

But that was as far as he got. Suddenly the pointer began to move. Meaty Guy's eyes shot down to it as it scooted across the board.

Scott swallowed a wave of uneasiness. The chill was back—licking up his spine, crawling over his skin.

The pointer continued to move, momentarily stopping over each letter until it spelled out the name:

B-A-R-T S-I-M-P-S-O-N

Meaty Guy stared at the board. "I don't get it. Bart Simpson isn't real. He's a cartoon character just like Fred—"

"It's a joke, stupid," Brooke said, pretending to laugh. Then, looking back to the board, she asked, "Helen, is that you? Helen of Troy, are you here?"

Immediately the pointer shot to the word *Yes.*

"That's Helen of Troy," Brooke explained. "She's got a great sense of humor."

"A regular Robin Williams." Scott smirked.

There were a couple more chuckles from the back, but Brooke ignored them.

"Helen," she called, "we have an unbeliever

in our midst. Is there someone he can talk
to—one of your friends who can help him
achieve greater enlightenment?"

The pointer rested silently.

"Helen? Are you still here?"

Again no movement. Nothing.

"Helen?" Brooke repeated. "Is there someone here who can make him a believer?
Please, tell us. Anybody?"

Then, ever so slowly, the pointer began to
move. All eyes watched as it gradually
spelled out the letters:

H-I-S

Then it stopped.

Brooke looked at Scott. "'His'?" she asked.
"Do you know anyone who calls himself
'His'?"

Scott shook his head, trying not to smile.
Things were already falling apart, and they'd
barely started. This was easier than he'd
thought it would be.

"Maybe they're initials," the redhead
offered. "You know, somebody with the initials H. I.—" She stopped as the pointer
started moving again. The letters came
much faster this time:

F-A-T-H-E-R

"'Father,'" Meaty Guy exclaimed. "His father?"

Brooke looked up to Scott. "Is that true? Is your father dead?"

Scott felt the chill spread across his shoulder blades and into his chest. He gave a little shudder. "Well, yeah, sure, but anybody could know that."

Brooke nodded and closed her eyes again. "Helen . . . Helen, will his father speak to us?"

Scott shifted uneasily. Somewhere, in the back of his neck, a dull ache began.

But there was no answer.

"Helen?"

The pointer started to move again. All eyes watched as it spelled out the letters:

H-E-L-L-O S-O-N

Scott took another swallow. "You're going to have to do better than that." He tried to smile, but he couldn't quite pull it off.

"What was his name?" Brooke asked.

"Uh, Hubert," Scott lied. Actually his dad was named after the apostle Paul.

Brooke turned back to the board and closed her eyes. "Hubert, tell us, what—"

Before she could finish, the pointer moved again.

P-A-U-L

Scott sucked his breath in as though he'd been punched in the gut.

Brooke opened her eyes. "Your dad's name isn't Hubert. It's Paul."

Scott's heart started to pound in his ears. The ache in his neck crept into his head and up to his temples. He took a deep breath and tried to relax. "Yeah, I, uh, I guess it is."

For the first time since they met, the slightest trace of a smile formed on Brooke's lips. "You still don't believe, do you?"

Scott searched for a snappy comeback but couldn't seem to find one.

"Ask him a question," the redhead said to Scott. "Ask him something only the two of you would know."

Scott's heart pounded louder in his ears. His head throbbed. It was getting hard to think. He knew he had authority over these guys, he knew he could win . . . but how, where to start . . . ?

"Go ahead," Darryl spoke up. "Ask him something."

"OK," Scott said, nervously clearing his throat, "All right . . ." Everyone waited as he thought. Finally he had it. "If you're really my father . . ." He took another breath. "If you're really my father, tell me what happened to my Swiss army knife."

It was a trick question. The Swiss army knife was actually his dad's. Scott had bought it for him last Father's Day, but Scott fell so in love with it that he constantly borrowed it from his dad. It had become a joke between the two of them . . . until his father's death.

The pointer went into action and quickly replied:

N-O-T Y-O-U-R-S . . .

Scott's jaw dropped as the answer continued to form:

M-I-N-E

A lump grew in his throat. Before he knew it, Scott's eyes began to burn. Could it be . . . ? No one else would have known. Not Mom. Not Becka. No one. Was it possible?

For the past six months, he had longed for his father . . . but it was more than a longing. It was an ache. An ache that went all the way into his gut. And nothing, absolutely nothing could ease it. Oh sure, he made his little jokes and pretended to have a good time, but underneath, the pain was always there. The man he adored, the man who had been the center of his life, had been suddenly and violently ripped away from him. And for six months, the pain had been unbearable.

But now . . .

At last Scott spoke. His voice was thick, barely audible. "Dad?" He reached out to the table to steady himself. "Dad . . . is it . . . is it you?"

The pointer quickly spelled:

T-E-L-L M-O-M A-N-D B-E-C-K-A . . .

The letters continued to form, but Scott's eyes were filling with moisture so quickly that it was hard to see. He tried to blink back the tears, but they only came faster. By now his heart thundered in his ears. His head throbbed unbearably. His father was there, somewhere in the room, trying to communicate. His father, the one he thought he'd never ever see again, was right there . . . spelling out the words:

I M-I-S-S Y-O-U G-U-Y-S.

"Oh, Dad—" The phrase caught in Scott's throat. He choked back a quiet sob. He couldn't help himself. He tried to speak again, his voice hoarse with emotion, just above a whisper. "I miss you, too . . . so much . . ."

And then, ever so gently, the pointer came to a stop.

Scott looked on, waiting for more.

But there was nothing.

"Dad." His voice carried a trace of panic. "Dad, don't go."

No answer.

"Dad . . . Dad, come back!" He was much louder. Practically shouting. "There's so much we don't know . . . Dad!"

Brooke turned to him. Her own eyes had a glint of moisture in them. "I'm sorry, Scott. He's gone."

"Dad," Scott desperately scanned the room, "Dad! Dad, don't go! Dad! Please come back! *Daaad!*"

But there was no answer. No movement on the board, no sound in the room. Only the uneasy cough of one or two kids. Everyone felt for him. Some looked to the ground in embarrassment. It's true, they'd won. They'd proven the board's power. But at the moment, no one felt like celebrating.

Scott's voice was fainter now, weaker. "Dad . . ." He angrily wiped at the tears spilling onto his cheeks.

But there was no answer.

9

"I can't believe you thought it was Dad!" Rebecca said as she paced back and forth in Scott's room. Mom had gone to bed hours ago, but they hadn't. The day had been brutal for both of them, and they were still up in his room comparing notes.

Cornelius sat on his perch, sound asleep.

"You had to be there," Scott insisted. "The Ouija board knew things."

"Like?"

"Like Dad's name, like that he died, like—"

"Scotty, anybody could have known——"

"Like the Swiss army knife I gave him for Father's Day."

Becka slowed her pacing and turned to him. "It knew that?"

Scott nodded. He slumped down in front of the computer. After a lengthy silence, he punched up Z's number. Maybe he'd have some more info.

Becka also had to sit. Slowly she eased herself onto the bed. She missed Dad as much as Scott did. She still cried, usually at the most inconvenient times. It didn't take much to set her off, just some little memory or some little phrase Dad had used, and suddenly, against her will, there were the tears. "How . . ." She cleared the thickness in her voice. "How could it be Dad when the Bible says . . ." Her voice trailed off.

"I know," Scott sighed. "The Bible says we die one time, then go to face God. No dead souls haunting houses, no dropping in for late-night seances. But it also says we're supposed to beat the bad guys." He hesitated a moment, then continued. "I gotta tell you,

Beck, after today I'm not sure what I believe."

Becka threw him a look. What was he saying? That the Bible was wrong? That he didn't trust it?

Feeling her eyes on him, he shrugged. "I call them like I see them. You get clobbered. I get clobbered. Then I wind up talking to Dad. Doesn't sound like what we've been told is all that accurate, does it?"

Rebecca took a long, deep breath and slowly let it out. All of their lives they'd been taught the Bible was true . . . but that was before Dad had died, before Becka had become the laughingstock of the school, before Scotty started getting beat up, before Dad started talking through Ouija boards. Maybe they were wrong, maybe the Bible wasn't—

NO! Becka pushed the thought out of her mind. Impossible. She refused to think it.

"Nothing from Z tonight," Scott said as he shut down the computer. "Well, I guess we'd better hit the hay."

Becka nodded and rose from the bed. "Sweet dreams," she said half sarcastically.

"Yeah, maybe I'll have another crazy one about Dad and his suit of armor."

Becka stopped at the door. "You've been dreaming about Dad?"

Scott nodded. "We're always playing football. And he's always wearing this suit of armor."

"Armor?"

"Weird, huh?"

"Not for you, Scotty." She sighed. "Nothing's too weird for you."

He nodded. "See you in the morning."

She stepped into the hall, hesitated, then turned back. "You know, Dad used to talk about armor."

Scott looked to her.

"Yeah," she continued. "Remember? 'Put on the whole armor of God.' He used to tell us that, remember?"

A scowl crossed Scott's face. "He did, didn't he?" He walked over to the shelf near the door and picked up his Bible. "Do you remember where that was?"

"Here let me." She took the book from his hands and quickly riffled through the pages. "Ephesians something . . ."

Scott's mind churned. Wasn't that what the dreams kept saying? 'Put on the armor, put on the armor'?

"Ah, here we go." Becka finally found it. "Ephesians 6:11. Listen: 'Put on all of God's armor so that you will be able to stand safe against all strategies and tricks of Satan.'"

Scott nodded. Satan was definitely pulling

some tricks, all right. But what kind of armor was it talking about? "Is there more?" he asked.

She continued: "'For we are not fighting against people made of flesh and blood, but against persons without bodies—the evil rulers of the unseen world. . . .'" Rebecca quietly groaned.

"What's wrong?" Scott asked.

"It's the way I treated Julie, like she was the enemy. But she's not. She's the one I'm trying to *save* from the enemy."

Scott nodded, but his mind was already on something else. "Read that last part again."

Becka backed up and repeated: "'For we are not fighting against people made of flesh and blood, but against persons without bodies—the evil rulers of the unseen world, those mighty satanic beings and great evil princes of darkness who rule this world; and against huge numbers of wicked spirits in the spirit world.'"

"Of course," Scott quietly whispered. "Why didn't I see it?"

Becka looked to him, not understanding.

He talked slowly, piecing it together as he spoke. "If we're fighting against all these evil spirits . . . and if they're all around . . . don't you think at least one of them would have known about that army knife?"

Becka frowned. "Run that past me again?"

"If these demons are everywhere, then one of them must have heard me and Dad joking about the knife back in Brazil, back when he was alive."

Rebecca began to nod. "Then it wasn't Dad talking through the board."

Scott nodded. "It was a demon, just like we thought . . . just like the Bible says."

They looked at each other a long moment before Rebecca turned back to the page and continued reading: "'So use every piece of God's armor to resist the enemy whenever he attacks, and when it is all over, you will still be standing up.'"

"We know that." Scott sighed impatiently. "But what does it mean by armor? What type of armor?"

"Hold it," Becka called as she silently read ahead, "there's more. Listen to this: 'In every battle you will need faith as your shield to stop the fiery arrows aimed at you by Satan.'"

"Shield?" Scott nearly shouted. "You said 'shield'!"

"Yeah—" Becka nodded toward the verse. "—'faith as your shield.'"

"That's it!"

"What's it?"

"Just like in the dream," he continued. "I

didn't have my shield in that bookshop, so I got clobbered, just like in the dream!"

"What are you talking about?" Becka demanded. "You have faith; you have a shield."

"No." Scott spun around to her. "I put my faith in what that Ouija board said. When I was there, the board convinced me I was talking to Dad. I believed what the board said instead of what the Bible said. I let down my faith—I dropped my shield."

"And got clobbered."

"Exactly," Scott exclaimed. "In the dream, it was physical with the football players, but in the Bookshop, it was spiritual."

Becka began to nod.

"Go ahead," he said, motioning toward the Bible. "Is there more? Anything else about armor or shields or anything?"

She read on: "'And you will need the helmet of salvation and the sword of the Spirit— which is the Word of God.'"

"Yes!" Scott could barely contain himself. "Just like in the dream!"

Becka looked back at him.

"Don't you get it?" Scott grabbed the book out of her hands. "This is our sword. This is what we fight with. We don't just win 'cause we're Christians. I strolled in there like some hot shot, thinking 'cause I was a Christian everything would go my way. But we have to use our shield and our sword. We have to believe God—that's our shield—and we have to use his Word," he said, waving the Bible, "our sword!"

Rebecca nodded, then she smiled. He was right.

"Isn't that incredible!" Scott cried. "It was all right here, right here! All we had to do was read it!"

Again Scott lay flat on his back in the middle of the football field. It was another dream, only this time he was wearing armor—just like his father's.

"Glad you finally suited up." His dad chuckled as he reached down and pulled him back to his feet.

"It took me a while to catch on." Scott grinned. "I tell you, for my imagination, you were sure vague about all this."

"Not really." His dad slapped him on the shoulder plate. "It's right there in the Playbook; you just had to be reminded." With that, the man turned and headed toward the locker room.

"Hey," Scott called after him, "where you going?"

"The game's over. You learned your lessons."

110

"But what about those kids?" Scott motioned toward the other team. "What about the members of the Society?"

"What do you care? You've got the truth now; that's all that counts."

The man had a point. Why should Scott care? He'd learned his lesson. He'd learned the truth. What difference did it make what they thought? After all, these were the kids responsible for locking him in the locker, for hitting him in the head with the baseball. If they wanted to fool around with fire, let 'em get burned. What did he—

And suddenly he saw them, over at the line of scrimmage. But this time the shadows were gone, and they were no longer giants. Now they looked like frightened kids— Meaty Guy, the redhead, even Brooke, the leader. They were all huddled together and seemed to be searching the field for someone . . . for anyone.

Suddenly the words Becka spoke earlier rang in his ears. *"They're not the enemy . . . they're victims of the enemy."*

He tried to ignore the thought; he tried to look away. But for some reason he couldn't. Then slowly, one after another, the faces turned toward him. Meaty Guy, Brooke, the redhead. Soon all their eyes were locked on his. They almost seemed to be pleading, to be begging. They didn't want to play any-more. It was obvious. They wanted to stop the game; they wanted to go home.

"Dad," Scott called, unable to take his eyes from the kids. "Dad . . . someone needs to tell them. They need help."

"You just want to show off again." His dad laughed lightly.

"No, I'm serious."

The man continued walking away.

"Please! I want to help. I mean that."

The man came to a stop, but he did not turn to face his son.

"They need someone to tell them," Scott repeated. "I know I was all full of pride, I know I was showing off before, but . . . just look at them."

The man still did not turn.

A tightness formed in Scott's throat. He wasn't sure if it was anger at his dad or pity for the kids. Maybe it was both. "Will you look at them!" he shouted. "They've got to be warned!"

The man still did not move.

"Aren't you listening?!" Scott cried. "Don't you care?!"

And then, ever so slowly, the man turned. There was a faint twinkle in his eyes. He began to nod. Scott wasn't sure, but somehow it felt like he'd just gone

through another test—only this time he
had passed.

"How?" Scott stammered. "What can I do?
How can I help?"

The man looked on saying nothing.

"Please," Scott said, "tell me straight, no
riddles, this time, just . . . tell me."

His father opened his mouth. He said
only one word. But it was enough. "Prayer."

Scott shot up in bed—wide-awake. He
wasn't covered in sweat this time, but he was
filled with determination.

~

"Becka, Becka wake up."

"Umph rommle raaur sa mophma. . . ,"
she mumbled. She was trying to say, "It's
4:30 in the morning—leave me alone,
jerkface," but at the moment, "Umph
rommle raaur sa mophma" was the best her
mouth could come up with.

Twenty minutes later, the two of them
were in her room with their Bibles open and
were poring over every verse they could find
about prayer.

"This is it!" Scott finally cried. "I knew it
was here." He began to read: "'And I tell you
this—whatever you bind on earth is bound
in heaven, and whatever you free on earth
will be freed in heaven.'"

"'Bind,'" Rebecca repeated, "like tie up?"

"Yeah." Scott nodded. "Like demons or spirits."

"And whatever we free?"

"Probably like angels and God's power and stuff."

Rebecca nodded.

"There's more. Listen: 'I also tell you this—if two of you agree down here on earth concerning anything you ask for, my Father in heaven will do it for you.'"

Rebecca shook her head.

"What's wrong?"

"How could we have been so stupid . . . to try and do all this stuff without even praying?"

"Well we're not stupid any more. What time do you have?" Scott asked.

"Almost six."

"Then let's get to it."

"To what?"

"There's two of us, right?"

"Right."

"And it says, 'if two of you agree on anything . . .'"

"You want to start praying for the Society?" Rebecca asked incredulously.

Scott nodded. "the Society, Julie, your friends, everybody—binding the spirits that are trying to hurt them and loosing God's power to protect them."

114

Rebecca gave him a look. "That's a lot of praying."

"You read it yourself. That's where the power is."

Becka hated admitting when Scott was right, but the guy had a point. A major point. "Well," she said, taking a deep breath, "let's get started."

10

hings turned
for the worse. All day Julie avoided Becka.
Word quickly spread around school that the
two friends had become enemies . . . that
Becka had used Julie, that she had become a
traitor, that she had taken everything Julie
had taught her in track and was planning to
turn it against her that afternoon at the big
meet.

So much for answered prayer, Becka thought. She almost wondered if it would have been better not to pray.

Almost, but not quite.

It seemed those verses about believing and not dropping her shield of faith kept rattling inside her head. So she kept praying. She prayed for Julie when the girl ignored her in the hall. She prayed when Julie's lunch table was suddenly "filled up." And now she said a silent prayer as she sat on the ground stretching and warming up for the 1600 meter race.

"Lord, please help Julie . . . show her your love, help her understand that—"

"All right, Becka, where is it?"

Rebecca glanced up. Julie hovered over her with her hands on her hips.

"Where's what?"

"Don't play innocent with me," Julie said with a scowl. "What did you do with my good luck charm?"

"What did I—"

"I put it in my basket when I suited up, and now I can't find it. Where is it?"

"Julie," Becka rose to her feet. "I haven't seen it."

"Don't lie to me!"

"All right ladies," said the woman at the check-in table. "Let's head on up to the starting line."

All the girls rose from the nearby benches and began to pull off their warm-ups. All the girls, including the three from Royal High . . . the three who planned to sweep the long distant events. Julie glanced over at them and swallowed hard. These were the people she wanted to beat. These were the people she *had* to beat.

They moved upfield toward the starting line—but Julie wasn't done with Becka. Not by a long shot. "Everybody knows you have it in for me, that you want to bump me out of getting to State."

Becka started to argue, but Julie would not be interrupted. "Where is my charm?" There was no missing the tremor in her voice.

"I haven't seen it," Becka insisted. "Honest."

Julie searched her face. "Becka, if you're lying . . ."

"I'm *not* lying. Could you have dropped it? Did you leave it with your sweats?"

"I've checked—I've checked everywhere!" Julie was starting to panic. "I need that charm."

"Julie, you're a better runner than me; you're better than all of us. You don't need some stupid—"

"You don't understand, I've never run without it!"

Becka looked at her, surprised.

Julie shrugged. "It sounds dumb, I know, but I need it. Becka, I . . ." She searched for the words. "I just need it!"

Becka felt herself growing angry, but not at Julie. She was angry at the charm. She was angry because it was turning her gifted friend into a quivering pile of self-doubt. There was nothing magical about that charm. It had no power. Becka looked at Julie again, and her eyes narrowed. Then again, in one sense, maybe it did. In one sense, Julie had given it so much control over her life that she might actually lose the race without it.

They approached the line. The starter—a man in a white shirt, black pants, and red blazer—motioned them forward. The best runners from five different schools, including the dreaded trio from Royal, stepped onto the track.

"All right ladies, listen carefully, because I'm only going to explain this once. . . ."

As the starter gave last-minute instructions, Becka shot a glance at Julie. The poor girl's eyes darted nervously about. No way was she concentrating. No way was her mind on the race. It was on that stupid charm. Finally Becka leaned over and whispered, "Focus."

Julie took a deep breath and nodded, but

Becka could tell when her friend looked over to the runners from Royal her mind resumed spinning.

"You can do it," Becka whispered. "Focus, just like you told me. You and me, Numero Uno, all you have to do is—"

"Excuse me, miss?"

Becka looked up. The man was glaring directly at her. "Am I interrupting anything?" he asked.

Becka shook her head and croaked, "Sorry."

"All right, let's get going then. Any questions?"

There were none.

The starter crossed to the end of the line and cleared his throat. "Runners to your mark."

Everyone stepped up to the line, taking last-minute breaths, shaking out last-minute tensions. Everyone but Julie. She was as tight as a fiddle string.

The man raised his pistol.

Becka caught Julie's eye. She mouthed the word, "Focus."

Once again Julie nodded and took a breath.

"Runners set . . ."

Everyone crouched, preparing.

Please, Jesus, Becka prayed.

And the pistol fired.

~

Scott stood all alone in the hallway of the Bookshop. He had not told Darryl. He had not told anyone. All he had were the words of Scripture, the prayers he and Becka had prayed that morning, and his faith. Was that enough? He'd soon find out.

He reached out and knocked on the door.

There was no answer.

He knocked again, louder.

Still no answer.

Fighting off another shiver, he asked God to be with him, to protect him. Then he took the knob, turned it, and quietly pushed open the door.

There was the usual darkness, the usual candles, the usual kids sitting around—half a dozen on the sofa, four or five around the Ouija board. They glanced up as he entered. A few started murmuring.

Meaty Guy scoffed. "Well, look who's back. Didn't you get enough yesterday?"

There were a few chuckles.

"No." Scott cleared his throat. "I mean, yes. I mean—" He took a breath and started over. "Look, I just want to let you know that what you're doing here, well, it's pretty dangerous."

"For who?" the redhead teased.

Scott let the dig go. "All I'm saying is that these demons are—"

"Spirits," Meaty Guy corrected. "Departed spirits."

Scott continued. "These demons are playing for keeps. You think you're using them, but they're really using you. They want to hurt you; they want to—"

"And you've come to save us?" Meaty Guy asked in mock seriousness. "To show us the light?"

Suddenly Scott remembered how much he disliked this guy. Suddenly he wanted to yell, "That's right, scum bucket! I have the light! I have the power! Stand back and let your puny brain be amazed!" But he pushed the urge aside. He remembered the faces on the football field; he remembered why he came.

To help.

"No." Scott shook his head. "I just came to tell you that what you're doing is—"

Suddenly he stopped. Something was happening. Brooke, the leader, hadn't said a word since he'd entered the room. In fact, she'd sat there the whole time, patiently waiting, with her eyes closed. But not anymore . . .

At first her movement was slight, like gentle swaying. But now her entire body started to shake.

"Uh-oh," Meaty Guy said, "here we go again."

Tension swept through the group. Suddenly Brooke's eyes flew open. She looked directly at Scott, but not with her usual self-assured arrogance. She was looking at him with desperation . . . and terror.

The shaking increased. Her hands slid off the table, and she knocked the pointer to the floor.

"Somebody give me a hand," Meaty Guy shouted as he rose and crossed to her. He grabbed her by the shoulders and tried to hold her down in the chair.

"Brooke!" he shouted. "Brooke, can you hear me?!"

She didn't answer.

Other kids were on their feet, quickly moving to help.

"What's going on?" Scott called.

"It's Joan!" Meaty Guy yelled. He did his best to hold Brooke down, but she grew more violent by the second.

"Who?"

"Joan of Arc," the redhead shouted. "She doesn't come often, but when she does, look out!"

Scott started forward then hesitated. He had to be certain.

The redhead continued to explain. "Joan

is so powerful she doesn't use the Ouija board to communicate. She talks right through Brooke."

That was it! Now Scott was sure. He'd seen this sort of thing before, back in Brazil, when the natives took their drugs, when they called on the demons to enter their bodies and take control.

The shaking had turned to violent lungings and lurchings. Sometimes Brooke would pull the entire chair into the air with her. They could no longer hold her. She was too wild. Too strong. She twisted and squirmed until she broke from their grasp and crashed to the floor.

"Brooke!" they shouted, "Brooke, can you hear us!?"

But if Brooke heard, she could not answer. Faint cries came from her mouth, but they were unintelligible, more like muffled screams. She writhed and thrashed and rolled on the floor like a madwoman.

"Stand back!" Meaty Guy yelled. "Let her go!"

Everyone stepped back. They yanked the chairs and table away so she wouldn't bang into them.

Scott had seen enough. "No!" he shouted. "Stop it!"

Everyone looked up startled. But he

wasn't shouting at them. He was shouting at Brooke.

"Don't worry," Meaty Guy yelled. "It'll be over in a minute."

"No!" Scott repeated to Brooke. "Stop it!" But nothing happened. "I said stop it!"

Still nothing.

"In the name of Jesus, stop!"

Immediately the thrashing slowed. Not a lot, but enough. If Scott had had time to think, he probably would have stopped. After all, shouting this sort of stuff wasn't the coolest thing in the world. Fortunately, he didn't have the time to think about being cool. "In the name of Jesus Christ," he repeated, "I command you to stop! Leave her alone!"

Meaty Guy started to protest, but there was something about the look in Scott's eyes that told him it wouldn't be smart to try and stop him. Scott stood directly over the girl and shouted, "In the name of Jesus Christ, I bind you! I command you to leave her. Now!"

No response.

"NOW!"

The writhing stopped. Instantly. One minute Brooke was a wild animal, the next she was totally normal—well, except for the heavy breathing, the sweat-drenched body, and the exhaustion. Her dyed black hair was thrown in all directions. Her cheeks and chin were wet with saliva. But she was back in control. Slowly she raised herself up to all fours, still panting.

Scott gently knelt at her side. Her hair hung over her face so he couldn't see it. He wasn't sure what to say, what to do, but he knew he had to explain it to her, he had to offer some comfort. He stretched out his hand to brush her hair aside, when suddenly she sprang at him, snarling like a wounded animal.

Kids screamed, and Scott jumped back. Brooke missed him by an inch. She hit the ground hard and resumed rolling and squirming and thrashing.

Scott sat on the floor, looking on in disbelief.

"See what you're doing!" Meaty Guy shouted at him. "You're making it worse!"

Scott looked up to him. For a moment he almost believed the guy. Then he remembered his dream. He remembered the Scriptures. He would not drop his shield. He would not put his faith in this kid or in what he saw on the floor in front of him. He would put his faith in God's Word.

Whatever you bind on earth is bound in heaven.

Scott jumped back to his feet and raced to Brooke. He stood over her and pointed. "I command you to leave her alone!"

Brooke's body tensed.

"In the name of Jesus Christ, I command you to leave!"

Suddenly a long, shrieking cry came from the girl's mouth. When it was over she collapsed, all her energy gone.

Scott stood over her, panting, catching his own breath. He sensed it was real this time. Whatever had taken control of Brooke had left. The room was silent.

Finally one of the girls approached Brooke. She knelt down and helped her sit up. Another joined them. Carefully they wiped her mouth and helped her over to the sofa. No one spoke. The only sound was Scott's and Brooke's labored breathing.

Nearly a minute passed before Scott spoke. "Look . . . I wasn't trying to show off here. But . . . well, you can see for yourself how dangerous—"

"Leave."

All eyes turned back to Brooke. "I'm sorry?" Scott looked at her, puzzled. It was her voice and she was back in control, but she didn't seem to be making any sense. "What did you say?" he asked.

"You are not welcome here," she answered hoarsely.

"I'm only trying to help."

"We don't need your help."

Scott stared at her in amazement. "What are you talking about? Don't you know what happened? Don't you know how that thing took control and threw you all over the—"

Brooke interrupted. Her voice was weak, but it was determined. "The greater the power I have, the greater the price I must pay. Now go."

Was she serious? After all that had happened? Scott glanced at the other kids. Most would not look at him. None would speak.

He turned back to Brooke. "You can't be serious."

Brooke nodded to Meaty Guy. "Show him to the door."

Meaty Guy hesitated.

"Now."

Scott held up his hand. "No. If you want me to go, I'll go. But you've got to see that—"

"We see more than you think, Scott Williams," Brooke said. "You are not welcome. Now go."

Again Scott looked at the faces of the group. They were kids, lots of them younger than he was. He wanted to help. He wanted to show them the dangers. But now . . . after all they'd seen, after all they'd experienced, and they still wanted to continue? Yet if this was what they wanted, there was nothing he could do. Demons he could command. But not people. People could do what they wanted.

Sadly, Scott turned and headed toward the door. When he arrived, he looked back at the group one last time. They were as helpless and pitiful as in his dream. There was so much more he wanted to say, so much more he wanted to do. But they'd made their decision.

Scott turned and stepped into the hallway. They shut the door behind him.

11

Halfway through the first lap, Becka knew her friend was in trouble. Like always, Julie pulled away from the group of runners early.

But this time there was a problem.

This time the trio from Royal had also pulled away from the pack. And now they were pulling away from Julie. With every stride they took, they moved farther and farther ahead of her. The reason was obvious. Even from Becka's position, back in the pack, she could see that Julie's concentration was gone. Totally. Instead of her easy, graceful strides, Julie was pumping and fighting and struggling. Instead of a fluid body that glided across the track, she was all elbows and knees.

Come on, Julie, Becka thought, *Concentrate. . . . Focus.*

By the end of the first lap, it was worse. Julie was a dozen meters ahead of Becka and the pack, but she was over a dozen meters behind the kids from Royal. Even with three laps to go, it appeared the race was over. Once again Royal High would take the 1600. Once again Julie would be bumped out of a chance to go to State. Everyone knew it.

Everyone but Rebecca.

As they started the second lap, Becka clenched her jaws in steeled determination. She took several deep breaths. And then, to everyone's amazement, Rebecca Williams began to sprint.

Coach Simmons looked on in disbelief. "Not now!" she yelled. "It's too early! What are you doing?"

But Becka knew exactly what she was doing. She knew that if she started her sprint this early, she'd be too exhausted to finish. She knew that if she killed herself on this race, she'd have nothing left for the other races—she wouldn't qualify for anything. And yet, despite all of that, she still dug her cleats in and pushed harder.

She moved through the pack, passing one runner after another. At last she pulled to the front. Julie was still fifteen meters ahead; the three girls from Royal were thirty.

As they passed Coach Simmons, the woman shouted at Becka. "You're too early! You'll have nothing left!"

Becka paid no attention. She pressed on.

They finished the second lap. Julie's strides were as unfocused and clumsy as ever. Meanwhile, Becka methodically closed the gap between them, from ten meters, to eight, to five.

Up in the stands, Krissi sat with fifty or so other students, watching. "Look at that," she cried. "Becka's challenging her, just like at practice. I told you she was a user."

Philip, her boyfriend, nodded, but Ryan wasn't so sure. "I don't think so, Krissi," he said. "Look. . . ."

Gradually Becka eased up beside Julie. Now they ran side by side. Becka's lungs were beginning to hurt again. She could never go the remaining two laps at this pace, but that didn't matter.

Julie glanced at her. There was no missing the fear in her eyes. But Becka was not challenging her. She neither pulled ahead of Julie nor dropped behind her. Instead she stayed right at her side.

Coach Simmons looked on in astonishment. She shook her head. Could it be? Was Becka doing what she thought she was doing?

Rebecca stayed glued to Julie's side. And then, through labored breathing, she began to shout:

"One! Two! One! Two!"

Her rhythm was rock steady, like a metronome.

"One, two, one, two . . ."

Back in the stands, Krissi demanded, "What's going on? What's she trying to prove?"

"I'm not sure," Ryan said, "but I think . . . I think Rebecca's pacing her."

"She's what?"

"She's giving her a count, a rhythm to follow."

Becka continued. Running at Julie's pace was hard enough. But to use up her air by counting out loud made it even harder.

"One, two, one, two . . ."

Gradually Julie fell into the rhythm. She began running with Becka, stride for stride.

Her concentration returned. Her fighting and struggling smoothed into the ease and grace for which she was known.

Becka continued counting, fighting for breath, "One, two, one, two . . ."

They moved ahead, the two of them together, gaining on the Royal runners.

"Atta girl!" Coach Simmons shouted. "Keep her steady, keep her steady!"

"One, two, one, two . . ."

They finished the third lap. One more to go.

Becka's throat was raw, like she'd worn a groove in her windpipe. Her lungs screamed for more air. She had never run at this pace for this long. Her arms were becoming dead-weight, her legs were turning to rubber. She could not go another lap. And still she counted:

"One, two, one, two . . ."

They passed the first runner from Royal. The girl looked up in shock and surprise. But there were still two more to go. It was time to pick up the pace. Becka knew Julie couldn't sprint, but they'd still have to move faster. Somehow, somewhere, Becka found the strength to push them ahead:

"One-two-one-two . . ."

They passed the second runner.

Becka stumbled, regained her balance,

and continued. Her head was light, her legs almost useless. She was losing control and she knew it. But she kept pushing.

Half a lap. Two runners down, one to go.

Becka stumbled again. Julie glanced at her in concern.

"Go!" Becka gasped. "Keep counting . . . faster!"

Julie picked up the cadence. "One-two-one-two . . ."

But it was over for Becka. Her legs had no feeling, no control. She had pushed them too far, and now, finally, they gave out.

She stumbled and lunged face first toward the track.

The crowd gasped as she hit the cinders and slid, as the red stones dug and slashed into her knees and arms. It was almost a repeat performance of her first day at practice.

Almost, but not quite.

She quickly staggered to her feet, gasping for air, looking toward the finish line. "Focus!" she shouted with her last ounce of energy. "Focus!"

It was doubtful Julie heard. She was concentrating too hard on the runner ahead. Inch by inch, she closed the gap. Thanks to Becka, she had found her rhythm. But more important, she had found the inspiration.

After all Becka had done, after all she had sacrificed for her, how could Julie let her down?

She couldn't. She wouldn't.

For the first time in her life, Julie reached deep into herself. And for the first time in her life, she found a sprint. It wasn't much . . . but it was enough.

OneTwoOneTwo . . .

Faster and faster she ran.

Ten meters to go.

Julie crept forward until she pulled along side the final Royal runner. The girl was so startled that her own concentration faltered.

That was all it took. Julie stretched out the last few strides.

Five meters. . . . Two meters.

She stuck out her chest, and with one final push, she hit the tape a fraction of a second before the girl from Royal.

The crowd went wild. They ran, shouting, onto the field. Julie staggered to a stop in their arms. She bent over, trying to catch her breath as the PA blasted out the time and announced the news, "That's a new District record, ladies and gentlemen. Julie Mitchell has just set a new District record!"

Spectators cheered. Team members hugged her and slapped her on the back. But Julie barely noticed. She was too busy looking through the crowd to the other side of the field.

There, Rebecca stood all alone—her hair messed, her knees raw and bleeding. The old Becka would have been embarrassed beyond belief. But, at least for now, this new Becka didn't care. For now, it was just the two of them on the field—no people shouting praises, no PA announcing records. Just two friends.

Slowly Becka raised her hand. Blood ran down her arm as she lifted her index finger. The gesture was simple, but Julie immediately knew what it meant.

"Numero Uno."

Julie returned the salute, raising her own hand, pointing her own finger. And as she did, her eyes filled with moisture. Tears spilled onto her cheeks. But they weren't tears of sadness or even tears of joy.

They were for Becka. They were tears of gratitude.

12

OTALLY RAD,
SQUAWK! TOTALLY RAD! TOTALLY RAD!"

Cornelius waddled across the desk as Darryl and Scott stared at the computer screen. The bird picked up a pencil in his mouth and began bobbing up and down with it, but no one paid attention.

"I'm still mad you didn't tell me you were

139

going to the Bookshop," Darryl squeaked in his usual high-pitched voice. "I wanted to see you do your stuff."

"I told you," Scott repeated, "I didn't go to put on a show."

"Just the same, everybody in the Society is pretty steamed."

Scott shrugged as he entered the chat room. "I was only trying to help."

As they looked at the screen, Darryl gave an unusually loud sniff. Scott threw him a look. By now the sniffing had really gotten on his nerves. He was thinking about giving the guy a gift certificate for tissues or maybe a lifetime supply of Dristan, when the information suddenly came up on the screen. It was another message from Z.

"This is that guy you were telling me about?" Darryl asked.

Scott nodded as he moved and clicked his mouse. "I'm not sure who he is, but he's, like, this real expert on—"

Suddenly Z's message came onto the screen. It wasn't long, but it definitely carried a wallop:

New Kid,
Congratulations on your victory. But remember, it is only the first battle. The war has just begun.
Z

140

Both boys stared at the screen. Darryl was the first to speak. His voice was higher and even more unsteady than usual. "How'd he know? It was just a few hours ago . . . how'd he know?"

Scott slowly shook his head. There was a lot about Z he didn't know. And what did he mean, "The war has just begun"?

"*SQUAWK*, MAKE MY DAY, MAKE MY DAY. . . ."

Cornelius was now jabbing at Scott's shoulder with a pencil he held in his beak. Scott reached over and scratched the nape of the little fellow's neck. The bird stretched his head in ecstasy, but Scott barely noticed. He was too busy staring at the screen, wondering.

~

"That's enough for now," Mom said, as they dumped the contents of another box from the garage into a plastic garbage can. "If we just do one or two of these a day, we'll get through them in no time," she said, wiping her hands.

Since they were together and since there was still some daylight, neither of them felt too uneasy about being in the garage. If they did, they didn't show it—except, of course, for their frequent glances toward the boxes at the far wall.

141

Becka hated the idea of being afraid of her own garage. It ticked her off. She was determined to get to the bottom of the mysterious light and sounds. And she would. Soon. Count on it. But not tonight. Tonight she was too bushed. The track meet had taken too much out of her.

Instead, she followed Mom into the kitchen, grabbed the garbage under the sink, and went back out to dump it into the second plastic garbage can. Then, with more than the usual grunts and groans, she dragged the two cans down the drive to the curb. Tomorrow was pickup day, and putting out the trash was one of her chores. She'd flipped Scott for that or for cleaning Cornelius's cage. And for once in her life she won.

Or so she thought . . .

"Need a hand with that?"

Becka looked up with a start. It was Ryan. Once again he had caught her hauling trash. Once again she was an unkempt sweatball.

"Oh, uh . . . hi, Ryan," she stammered as she instinctively straightened her hair (as if it would do any good).

He waited.

Remembering he'd asked a question, she frantically searched her mind. *What did he say? Something about helping? Oh, yeah.* "No, thanks," she replied. "I'm just setting these two garbage cans out on the curb."

He nodded.

What a stupid answer! she thought. *Of course I'm setting the cans out on the curb. Anybody can see that.* But Ryan didn't seem to notice her lapse of intelligence.

"Listen . . ." He coughed slightly. "I saw what you did out on the track this afternoon. It was pretty impressive." Becka started to protest, but he continued. "No, it was cool. And, uh . . . well, I'm sorry if we, you know, gave you a rough time or anything."

Becka shrugged. "It wasn't that bad," she lied.

He looked at her. Was it her imagination or were those blue eyes sparkling slightly?

Suddenly Ryan remembered something. He reached into his pocket and pulled out Julie's leather pouch. "She said it was in her gym basket all along—guess she just didn't see it." He held out the pouch to Becka. "It almost cost her the race, so she figures it's not so lucky after all. She said you'd know what to do with it."

Becka reached out and took the pouch into her hand. She wanted to say something, but once again her voice was on vacation . . . along with her mind. It was the same trip

143

they always took whenever this guy was around.

The silence grew. They both shifted slightly.

"Well, I, uh . . . I guess we'll see you tomorrow," he finally said.

"Yeah," Becka croaked. "Tomorrow."

Ryan turned and sauntered on up the street. Rebecca glanced back down at the charm in her hand. The charm. All that trouble over a leather pouch with a bunch of stupid rocks and stuff inside. Well, it was over now.

Without a further thought, she dropped it into the garbage.

"Oh, hey?" Ryan turned back to her. "I got tickets to this hot speaker coming to the library next week. The Ascension Lady gave them to me."

Becka looked at him.

He shrugged. "It's some reincarnation guy claiming to be Napoleon in some past life. Guess he's going to give a demonstration. Want to come?"

Rebecca continued to stare. She knew her mouth was hanging open, but there wasn't much she could do about it.

Ryan waited another second before continuing. "Well, think about it. Maybe you can let me know tomorrow." With that he turned and headed back up the street.

Becka closed her eyes. Could it be? Could this whole thing be starting all over? The Ascension Lady . . . ? Reincarnation . . . ?

Oh, brother, Rebecca thought, taking a deep breath and slowly letting it out. *Here we go again.*

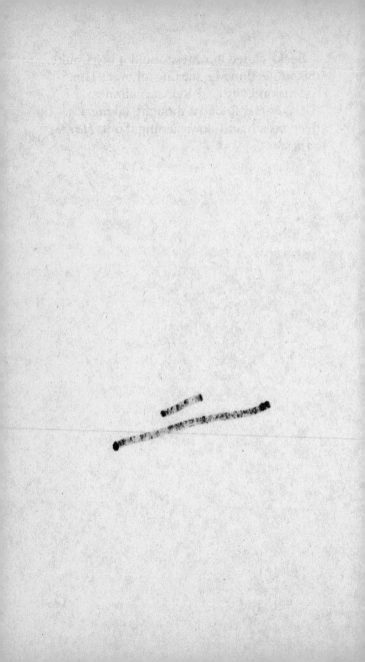

Information on the occult came from the following sources:

Pp. 58–59—Bill Myers, *Hot Topics, Tough Questions* (Wheaton, Ill: Victor Books, 1987) 91–93; *Understanding the Occult* (Minneapolis, Minn: Augsburg Fortress Pubs., 1989) 96.

Pg. 75—Edmond Gruss, *Cults & Occult in the Age of Aquarius* (Grand Rapids, Mich: Baker Book Pubs., 1974); see also Volney P. Gay, *Understanding the Occult* (Minneapolis, Minn: Augsburg Fortress Pubs., 1989) 96; Bill Myers, *Hot Topics, Tough Questions* (Wheaton, Ill: Victor Books, 1987) 91–93.

AUTHOR'S NOTE

As I continue writing this series, I have two equal and opposing concerns. First, I don't want the reader to be too frightened of the devil. Compared to Jesus Christ, Satan is a wimp. The two aren't even in the same league. Although the supernatural evil in these books is based on a certain amount of fact, it's important to understand the awesome protection Jesus Christ offers to all those who have committed their lives to him.

This brings me to my second and somewhat opposing concern: Although the powers of darkness are nothing compared to the power of Jesus Christ and the authority he has given his followers, spiritual warfare is not something we casually stroll into. The situations in these novels are extreme to create suspense and drama. But if you should find yourself involved in something even vaguely similar, don't confront it alone. Find an older, more mature Christian (such as a parent, pastor, or youth leader) to talk to. Let them check the situation out to see what is happening, and ask them to help you deal with it.

Yes, we have the victory through Christ, but we should never send in inexperienced soldiers to fight the battle.

Oh, and one final note. When this series was conceived, there were really no bad guys on the Internet. Unfortunately that has changed. Today there are plenty of people out there trying to draw young folks into dangerous situations through it. Although the characters in this series trust Z, if you should run into a similar situation, be smart. Anyone can *sound* kind and understanding, but their intentions may be entirely different. All that to say, don't take candy from strangers you see . . . or trust those you don't.

Bill

FORBIDDEN ● DOORS

Want to learn more?

Visit Forbiddendoors.com on-line for special features like:

- a really cool movie
- post your own reviews
- info on each story and its characters
- and much more!

Plus—Bill Myers answers your questions! E-mail your questions to the author. Some will get posted—all will be answered by Bill Myers.